A TASTE OF TERROR

Other books by Martha Albrand

A TASTE OF TERROR

by
Martha Albrand

G. P. PUTNAM'S SONS
NEW YORK

Cl 5.92

Copyright © 1976 by Hodder and Stoughton

All rights reserved. This book, or parts thereof, must not be reproduced in any form without written permission.

SBN: 399-11965-5

Library of Congress Cataloging in Publication Data

Albrand, Martha.
  A taste of terror.

  I. Title.
PZ3.A3397Tas [PS3551.L28] 813'.5'2 77-3446

For my friends Waria and Hans

For aeronautic advice and help
I am indebted to Captain Bill Litwin

I

"THEY WILL HAVE to be killed," said my father. He turned
in the abrupt way he always did once he'd made up his
mind, and left me standing there in the snowy field,
staring at the ghastly sight. Our small flock of sheep had
been attacked by a wild dog. Twenty were dead, twelve
barely alive. The ram must have put up a terrific fight.
His beautifully turned horns were partly torn out and his
wounds were still bleeding profusely. He lay in the middle
of the meadow, while the ewes, in their efforts to escape,
were near the fence the dog — or dogs — must have
jumped, for the gate was closed, its lock unbroken.

Whenever we had been away from home for any length
of time, we always checked the animals — the cowbarn,
the chicken-coop, the two work horses in their stable under
the hayloft. Standing there in the bright moonlight that
made the snow seem even whiter, I cried.

My father came back. In his left hand he carried a
lantern, in his right his old army revolver. He handed it
to me. I shrank back in horror; I shook my head in
silent defiance. He shook his in response. "We've got to
put them out of their misery." His knowing hands went
over each animal, still writhing in pain. "And you have
to learn to do what is necessary. To allow needless suffering is a sin. What we can't do for humans, we can at
least do for animals. Here, get on with it." He pointed to
the main artery of old Eva. My hands shook. He said,
"Steady, boy." I pulled the trigger. I pulled it twelve
times, making my round among the bleeding sheep. Each
time there was a new spurt of blood, coloring the snow
a deep red. When it was all over, I vomited.

Back in the house, my father poured me the first drink
I'd ever had. Bourbon. It made me cough violently. My

father, who rarely drank, poured us a second. I began to cry again. "A man doesn't cry when he's done what is necessary. Go to bed now."

I went to bed but couldn't sleep. All my life it has been difficult for me to sleep during the first white nights when no pollution has yet touched the snow, and it lies like a soft white blanket, stretched out over hills and meadows. Usually I turned on the radio to distract myself, but this time nothing could distract me.

Since then there have been winters when the memory of that night was faint, faded into a nightmarish dream, but then its full impact hit me again. Again the snow was covered with blood, and people, writhing in pain, were scattered on the ground, dying, or already dead. It seemed like eternities until the fire equipment came and something could be done in the snow and ice that made the mangled bodies shapeless. I wished I had a revolver to shoot those who were beyond saving, but I had nothing with which to put them out of their misery. And most of all I wanted to kill the pilot. Like the savage dog who had attacked our sheep, he seemed to me to be the cause of their torment and death. Thomas J. Kent. Twenty of our sheep had died, the rest had had to be killed. Twenty of his passengers had died in that crash; he was one of the survivors, and all he suffered was a broken hip and ankle.

I don't know how often I have jotted down his name on scraps of paper or written it on a whole page, all by itself; said his name over and over again. Why do I hate him with the same murderous hate I felt for the dog? Because I think the investigation was wrong in clearing him of any responsibility for the crash? The dog owed nothing to our sheep, but Kent accepted the aircraft although he was apprehensive about the checks on the landing gear. To my mind he owed his passengers not only a quick but a *safe* arrival. But did he care if they arrived safely or not? Was he gambling with his life, without a thought for the lives of his passengers? To believe in fate is too easy. At least that's my opinion. Fatalism is too easy too. It can always find an excuse, a rationalization, for any situation. I loathe fatalists.

Maybe I don't make sense any longer. Frankly, I don't care if I do or not. And if there's no logic in my argument... there is no logic in emotions. For me Kent and the dog have become one. And I can't reconcile myself to the idea that he can get away with the death of twenty people, who, in my opinion, needn't have died if he hadn't been negligent, but the dog had to pay the penalty.

Oh yes, I killed the dog. I don't like to think of it. Sometimes it haunts me. But the truth is, I did. For weeks I sat on the fence of the cow pasture, walked around our small, one hundred and thirty-three acre farm, of which seventy acres were tilled, the rest woodland, watching, listening, waiting. And then, one day, I saw him. I think it was in March. A vicious wind was blowing and I was shivering in the damp cold. A mutt. Something between an Alsatian and a setter. Greyish, with some blond spots, its fangs bared. He fled the moment the wind carried my scent to him. From then on we outwaited each other. At the edge of the wood a little spring had managed to bore through the tough clay soil. He used to come there to drink, but now, for days, he didn't show. I knew he was hiding in the stone quarry, a spot I was afraid of because snakes liked it. My father — long since dead — thought it might hold some uranium and that one day we would be rich. We never were.

I had no darts that shot tranquilizers into your prey, but I had fashioned a lasso and practiced with it. One day the wind was with me and I let it go. I caught him all right. His two front legs, and God, was I proud of it! I dragged him toward me. He was barking wildly, desperately, but I pulled him mercilessly. The foam of anxiety was around his mouth and a pleading look in his big hungry eyes. I tied him to the nearest fencepost with a chain. I took the law into my own hands. Instead of just killing him, I tortured him, although I knew he hadn't tortured the sheep consciously, just fed on their blood and flesh and indulged his need to kill. I set fire to the root of his tail, I pulled out the nails of his front paws, I... never mind... did other things before I finally killed the ani-

9

mal. I didn't vomit then. I felt satisfied. I had taken my revenge for the death of our sheep.

I don't recall how long it took me to tell my father. He listened to me in silence, his eyes fixed on me unblinkingly as if he were in a trance, then he got up slowly, grabbed me by the scruff of the neck with one of his quick, abrupt gestures, and gave me a beating before he threw me out of the house into the pelting rain. "Of course, wild dogs have to be destroyed, but to torture . . ."

For a few days he wouldn't speak to me; he treated me as if I didn't exist. Then one morning, over breakfast, he said, "I want you to remember, son, that nobody has the right to take the law into his own hands. Don't ever forget that."

But times were different then. My torturing the dog did not make me feel guilty, nor did my father's words convince me that man was not justified, under certain circumstances, in exercising his own law. Not in our times, and I don't think I need to explain or enlarge on that. We all know only too well that justice has become something to sneer at. Murder, mugging, rape, often for no reason at all, are rampant, as if civilized man were something unheard of. And more often than not, these crimes go unpunished. As Thomas J. Kent has gone unpunished. I am therefore not opposed to taking the law into my own hands when nobody else will. Yet I shudder when I read the letter which I have composed in great agony. I have read it over and over again, hesitating to send it off. I hope I never will.

2

THOMAS J. KENT walked the short distance from house to fence where, at the gate, the red mailbox with his name on it showed where he lived. He was still on crutches and walking was difficult and at times painful. The break in his left hip with its comminuted fracture had been pinned, making him ambulatory almost immediately, but the ankle, broken at the end of the tibia, including the medial malleolus, was still in a cast. "No weight on your left foot for at least six, maybe eight weeks," the doctor had warned him, which had meant no flying until then.

There was no need for him to get the mail; Kitty or Kate would have done it gladly, but he had insisted on doing it himself. "You've got to let me do as much as I can," he had told them, and they had finally understood. Putting most of his weight on his right leg, he made it, slowly and determinedly, three hundred yards from the white, clapboard house, with about fifty curses in between. He had never been a patient man.

Zero, their Alsatian, named by Kate was jumping around him, looking for a chance, when his master's eye wasn't on him, to jump the fence to the neighboring property and chase cats, rabbits and birds. Once or twice Kent called out to him sharply, "Heel," but Zero had a mind of his own. While Kent took out the mail, he was off.

There had been a lot of mail, much more since the crash. Endless forms to fill out, from the insurance, from the line — and now there was only the usual junk mail. A few personal letters and bills. He shoved everything into the shoulderbag Kitty had given him when he had first started moving around on crutches, and it had become a rather messy file for letters to be answered, newspaper clippings, notes on what he wanted to read, bills that had to be paid, memos of things that had to be done around the house, Kitty's bank statement. How disorderly invalidism could make a man. But tonight Kitty had promised to empty the whole thing, sort it out and take care of whatever had to be attended to. Thank God for Kitty and her efficiency.

He noticed that Zero had gone, and whistled. Whistling still hurt, although his broken ribs had mended. Wherever Zero was, he evidently had no intention of obeying. Kent went back to the house, past the two-car garage, around the small garden shed in which Kate liked to sleep on hot summer nights or whenever she was feeling adventurous. He had put in two windows for her, and a door that locked securely. He reached the swimming pool, a small one, yet still it had taken a year of debating — should they put it in? Shouldn't they? Although he made a good salary, life had become expensive, what with the maintenance of the house, the two cars, Kate's dancing and riding lessons, and what he thought he owed some friends disabled in Vietnam who had been close to him in Pensacola. Exhausted, he sank down on one of the quite elegant lounge chairs. Kitty never bought anything cheap. Either they could afford it or they would wait until she could get what pleased her. He liked this trait in her. It made their surroundings beautiful but, at times, sparse. She had been the one who had decided, when they moved east for greater convenience, to live in King's Point. He'd laughed at what he called her romantic snobbish attitude, but for her it was Fitzgerald country and part of a period in which she would have liked to live. "The golden days" when the Bloomingdales, the Satterwhites, the Livermores, the Sloans, Swops and Chryslers and many others of the great families had owned such fabulous estates which now had mostly been broken up into developments or served as public buildings. No longer did people own several private tennis courts or give croquet parties at night, lighted up by the headlights of cars. Not that they had many friends, partly due to the uncertain hours of his profession which made attending parties or giving them inconvenient, but also because they liked to be by them-

12

selves and there was always New York, near enough to make it possible if not always for him, at least for Kitty to go to the theater or a concert and meet old acquaintances.

He stared at the pool. A slight film covered the water. He should throw in some chemicals, but shook his head. Kate would do it. He wondered why she hadn't already done so. But then she was in love with Abraham, an Arabian horse, and torn between Abraham and a boy called Jerry.

He took off his shoulderbag, and as if it had been a grabbag, reached in and drew out an envelope. A blue envelope. His name and address in red block letters. Red was a festive color, and he let it lie on his knees for a while before opening it.

It was written in the same red block letters as the envelope.

Thomas J. Kent. No matter that you have been acquitted of any guilt in the crash of your Boeing 727 — it was your negligence that killed twenty people and made life a torture for those who survived. No decent human being would go on living with the knowledge that he had caused such misery. But you seem to have no such sense of responsibility. We feel it is essential that you redeem yourself, and can see only one way in which you can do it. If you don't kill yourself in recognition of your guilt, we shall exercise the punishment you deserve on your daughter, Kate.

There was no signature.

The letter of a crazy man. Kent tore it up. Nuts, he thought, and lay back on the lounge chair, staring into the sky. Cloudless today. The first of May. Kate was like a May day, full of the promise of spring, blue-eyed like the sky, a pale, iridescent blue and softly warm. She should have been called Primavera, he thought, and suddenly the meaning of the red-inked letter struck him. "If you don't kill yourself . . . we shall exercise the punishment you deserve on your daughter . . ."

13

Frantically he retrieved the scraps of paper he had let fall beside his chair. Just then Kate appeared, her hand holding Zero's collar. "How did he get out? I locked him in. Really, Thomas..."

She had always called him by his first name instead of Dad or Pop, whereas she addressed her mother as Mom. He looked at her, fourteen years old, almost fifteen, slight, graceful, freckles across her nose, her eyes, as usual, bright.

"You're home early," he said. "How come? Your mother will be waiting in front of the school..."

Kate shook her head. Her hair was blond like his, like the first tender yellow of a willow. "Some kids attacked a teacher so all of us were sent home. Search me why. I called Mom at the hairdresser's. It's Tuesday, her day. Jerry's mother gave me a lift."

"Why was your teacher attacked? Which teacher?"

"History. Miss Marks. You know her. She made some remarks about the Republicans, and you know how it is out here — everybody dead-set against the Demos. And then — Miss Marks is black. I adore her."

Kent didn't feel up to a political discussion with his daughter. "Will you do me a favor," he said. "Get me some scotch tape from my desk."

She floated away. She moved like her mother, yet she was very unlike Kitty. Very unlike him. At Kate's age, they hadn't been so keenly involved in politics.

Kate came back from what she called his "cage", his small study on the second floor, just large enough to hold a trestle table and two chairs, a Sony, and of course the telephone. There were telephones all over the house so that he could be reached at any moment by the line. She pointed to the scraps of blue paper on his lap. "Is that what you want to put together again?"

He nodded, and she bent down and retrieved the envelope which had fallen under his chair. "Why did you tear it up if you wanted it whole again?"

"I thought it wasn't important."

There were only four pieces, so it was easy to make them fit together. He stuffed the scotch-taped sheet and the envelope into his jacket.

14

"It's unlike you not to notice at once what's important and what isn't."

"I'm not at my best yet."

"I know," said Kate. "But don't let it worry you. You wouldn't be human if you, who has never had an accident..." she shut up, and after a second shrugged. "Sorry."

"No need to be sorry," he said, getting up. "I'm over it. Emotionally, that is. Such things are unfortunately a part of life." He realized suddenly that walking along beside him, she was limping. He stopped abruptly. "Kate, there's something I want you to do."

"What?"

"Stop imitating people."

"I don't imitate people."

"Yes, you do. For weeks now you've been walking around like me, as if you had one foot in a cast. Whenever your mother twiddles her hair around a finger because she's puzzled about something, you do it too. And when Sam cracks his knuckles because he's excited, you start doing it. And the way you speak. I can always tell to whom you've been talking last because your voice takes on the same intonation, and often you use their expressions."

"I think that's quite natural," said Kate. "Look at animals, the way they change their feathers or pelts according to the seasons. It's a sort of self-protection."

"From what do you have to protect yourself?"

"From just being always me. Sometimes I do it because I can't help it, sometimes because I'm bored and it's sort of fun, but mostly I'm trying to pick up gestures and ways of speaking on purpose. If you want to be an actress..."

"Okay. But stop limping. It's painful for me to think that a girl your age might have to limp."

"But I could break a leg, fall off a horse; a car could hit Jerry's motor bike..."

"Possibly. But let's wait for you to limp until the occasion arises."

"But it's a sort of training."

15

"You'll be trained properly when the time for that comes."

"Strasberg mightn't be alive then."

"There are other teachers."

"Like the Royal Academy in London?"

"Perhaps."

As they walked toward the house, into it, through the kitchen, into the back hall and up the stairs, Kent was amused by her efforts to walk naturally, two steps ahead of him most of the time, then restraining herself and falling in with him, side by side.

"Want me to put a record on for you? The Bach Mom brought home for you yesterday? It always calms you."

"I'm perfectly calm. I don't want music right now."

But he wasn't calm, and it embarrassed him that Kate should have detected it. "Go and do your homework," he said. "And later, if Mom doesn't need you, I'll play some gin with you."

"For how much a point?"

"Maybe just for honor."

Kate made a face, wrinkling her nose like a rabbit. How primal the greed for money was in a child!

It was only when he sat down in the revolving chair in front of his desk to read the blue, red-inked letter again, that he noticed that it had dropped out of his pocket. He got up, looked down the staircase, saw it wasn't there, retraced his steps, through the back hall, the kitchen, across the small stone terrace, down the three steps to the swimming pool. Kate was in the water, nude except for the narrow strip of her bikini. The letter lay on the flagstones, a few feet away from where he had been sitting.

"Want me to get it for you?" she called out to him, apparently knowing what he had come back for.

Before he could shake his head, she was out of the water, bending to pick up the letter. How beautiful, he thought, distracted for a moment by her young body, pearly with drops of water, her long legs, tiny behind, no breasts yet, just small pink nipples. But then, children her age were usually a pleasure to look at unless they were

16

fat, like Jerry, or plain, like some of her other boy friends. "Why can't she find a good-looking guy?" he had asked Kitty once, and Kitty had laughed. "Because our daughter is a vain little bastard. It sets her off to be seen with less beautiful kids. She's not mature enough yet to be sure of herself."

"Thanks," he said politely, reaching for the envelope. "Isn't the water still pretty cool?"

Kate dived and came up at the other end, just as he passed it. There was something in the way she held her nose between her thumbs, shaking her wet hair, that made him stop suddenly. "Did you read it?"

"I know you're not supposed to read other people's mail."

"Well, did you or didn't you?"

Kate climbed up the few steps of the aluminum ladder where she had her towel, flung it around her so that only her legs were visible, shrugged, "You've often said people shouldn't tempt other people. Now if they leave a letter lying around . . ."

"I didn't leave it lying around. You saw me piece it together and put it in my pocket."

Her face went crimson, and the rising color made her eyes seem even lighter. "I read it."

Kent's heart seemed to miss a beat, but he said nothing. Kate stamped her foot. It made an eerie sound on the wet stone. "What does he want, Thomas? It's ridiculous to propose that you kill yourself to redeem . . . what the hell does he mean — redeem? For what? The NTBS concluded that the cause was mechanical failure. It was in all the papers. They said you'd done your job in the most professional manner. The ALPA even gave you a citation for your skill in handling the incident."

Kent's teeth set. He stared at his daughter. The new generation. How much their minds could grasp. Or was it simply loyalty to a beloved father that made Kate remember so precisely what she had read. But he didn't want to reflect on this now. What was important at this moment was what impression the threatening note had made on his daughter.

17

Before he could phrase the delicate question, Kate told him matter-of-factly, "I wouldn't pay any attention to it. It's the letter of a crazy man. Throw it away."

How much like her mother she was, fearless, dismissing all eventualities of violence or death. Perhaps she hadn't grasped the threat to her own security if he failed to comply to the preposterous demand.

"Don't worry about me," said Kate. "I'm very much aware of what can happen to kids since Rhoda was raped and Mom had me take up judo. I never walk near the curb where anyone can grab me and pull me into his car, and I keep away from doors and entrances when I'm in the city."

Suddenly he was absurdly relieved that Kitty had persuaded Kate to take a class in self-defence, and to see that Kate was in no way frightened by the threat to his life or hers. "Rather a tall order, isn't it?" she said, "to ask you to kill yourself to keep me from harm. Fuck him."

He didn't think he'd heard correctly. "That's what Jerry would say," she went on, "and if it's a word you'd rather I didn't use, just give me a better one. It's the only word that describes how I feel."

"Kate," he said, "just the same, I want you to promise me something."

"What?"

"You're not to breathe a word about this letter to your mother."

Kate shook her head to get some water out of her ears. "Why not?"

"It might worry her."

"Mom never worries."

It was true, and it was what made life with Kitty so delightful. But in this case he knew she would. "She might."

"But you share everything with her."

"It's an order," he said. "You're not to mention this letter to your mother, nor to anyone else."

"Not even to Sam or Jerry?"

"Not to anyone. It's time you learned to keep a secret, even if it upsets you."

18

"I'm not upset. If anything I'm outraged, that anyone should dare to . . ."

"I said, it's an order."

His voice, with its unaccustomed sternness, made her step back. "Yes, sir!"

He pushed the letter carefully into the pocket of his jacket. Kate said in a voice small with surprise, "But it worries you, doesn't it, Thomas?"

His throat went dry. He had achieved exactly the opposite of what he had set out to do. To spare Kitty any nightmarish thoughts he had planted apprehension in Kate's mind, had made her a part of his anxiety. Unpardonable. But, no, he told himself. It's better that she knows. Now at least she'll be more on guard. Of course, in the end Kitty will have to know too, but not yet, he thought. Not until I've got in touch with the F.B.I.

"You didn't answer me," Kate said. "I asked you if it worries you."

"It's just that I don't like crazy people," he said lightly.

"I do," said Kate. "They're much more interesting than a lot of stuffed shirts I know. And as Miss Marks says: who's normal? And what is normal? It's nothing but the code we choose to judge our fellow men."

"All right. But just the same, let's keep it a secret."

"And not let Mom in on it?"

"Right. Just between you and me."

Kate grinned. "Be my guest," she said, and dived back into the water.

Kate was enormously proud of her father. Not only had she read every word about him, listened to radio and television interviews, she had recently written a school paper on him. Twenty years old when he had left college and started at Pensacola Navy Flight Training Center. Finished two years later as an ensign and served after that in an operational squadron. Stayed four extra years in the navy and left as Lt. Commander. He had married her mother when he was twenty-six and they had stayed in Florida. Barely twenty-eight years old, he was accepted at the EAA as a pilot engineer. It was then that

Mom and Thomas had decided to have a child — me. Four years later he had become a co-pilot, got his rating — the highest license, Air Transport Rating — just on her birthday, the loveliest birthday present. And finally, Captain. Of course, Thomas had filled in all sorts of experiences and anecdotes, because he had thought her paper was too dry and not always accurate. And now I share a secret with him, she thought, and I'll keep it. He knows he can trust me.

She went to the diving board and tried a back-flip which she had been forbidden to do since the pool was too shallow for anything more than just an ordinary dive. Kent didn't see it because all of a sudden he knew what disturbed him most of all. Of course, there had been crank letters, hate mail and vindictive calls, as in almost every case after a crash. But they had been addressed to the line. This letter, however, had come to his home. No line gave out a pilot's home address. His name had of course appeared in the papers, but never his address. The writer of the letter therefore knew where he lived. And that he had a daughter named Kate. It had to be someone who knew him. Who?

He called the F.B.I. and made an appointment for the following morning.

3

SAM SLEW CAME by before Kitty got home from the hairdresser. Kent knew from the way Kate whistled for Zero, to lock him away. Sam didn't like Zero, nobody actually did, except Kate. Certainly not the neighbors, whose grounds he invaded whenever he got loose, chasing their cats and scratching up their flower beds, nor Kate's boy friends, who resented that he wouldn't let them touch Kate — a fact Kent liked — nor the old ladies who came to bake their cakes for church fairs in Kitty's big kitchen. "Because they smell," Kate had explained when the question had come up of getting rid of him because of the many complaints, "to high heaven of lavender soap." "Up in the cage," he heard Kate call out, and a moment later Sam knocked at the door of Kent's study.

Slew never came in without knocking, even if he'd been told he could walk right in. He was a man of heavy build, yet he managed to move with a certain grace that was peculiarly his own. Mostly he walked slightly tiptoe, as if he were afraid to put his full weight on his heels. There were other strange things about him which had made some people wonder if he wasn't perhaps a fag. Unmarried, with apparently no need of a woman to keep house for him, just a cleaning woman. A soft voice, certain movements of hands and hips. Still, no sign of a man around either. Kent liked him; he admired especially the skill of Sam's hands. There was nothing they couldn't fix. They were quite beautiful, perhaps the only beautiful feature about him, like leaves, fingers thinning from a strong palm that seemed to have a built-in antenna for finding out what was wrong with a pump, a motor, any mechanism. Long before they had moved to King's Point, Sam had started there as a handyman, working around private estates, then set up his own business, "Sam's Maintenance", and pretty well sewed up the neighborhood. There was hardly anyone who wasn't dependent on Sam's crew to cut lawns, trim trees and hedges, service swimming pools. The business had been too lucrative to give up when he had started as an independent contractor and made a success of that. Their house had been his first big assignment and he'd done a good job, reasonably too. The fact that he had been Kitty's friend years before Kent had met her may have had something to do with that.

"Thanks."

Sam sat down. "Thought you wouldn't mind...I brought up some beer." He lifted the bottlecap with the strong thumbnail of his right hand, a trick Kent had tried in vain.

"Just what I needed."

Kent was glad to see Sam. There was something so down to earth about him, it calmed one's nerves. Soon after they had met, Kent had discovered that Sam, like him, was a passionate fisherman, and he had invited Kent to join him for some fishing. Sam kept a motor-boat on the south shore. For Kent it had been the ideal relaxation, and he was looking forward to the day when he could go out with Sam again.

"You drink too much," Sam said, pointing to the nearly empty bottle of whiskey that stood next to Kent's phone. "No good, you know."

"I know," said Kent.

Sam frowned. Actually, he was always frowning. The sharp furrows rose from the root of his potato nose like a permanent scar. "Worried about your future?"

"Don't give it a thought."

It was true; he had had nothing to worry about until today.

"So what do you look so puked out for?"

Kent hadn't intended to show anyone but the F.B.I. the letter, but now he shoved it across the desk to Sam. Ever since they had become friends, he had relied on Sam's advice in many things and respected his judgment.

Sam's eyes, round like old-fashioned jet buttons and

usually expressionless, narrowed to slits as he read the letter. He shoved it back. "Shit."

"Quite possibly. But I can't dismiss it from my mind because of Kate."

"Then fuck yourself or kill yourself. It's your choice. When did you get it?"

"This morning."

"Forget it."

Kent was relieved to find Sam's reaction the same as his, when he had first read the letter. Still he said, "Can't. There are too many crazy guys around in the world we live in."

"What makes you so sure it's a man? It isn't signed."

Kent stared at Sam, his eyes wide. "It never occurred to me that anybody but a man ... didn't occur to Kate either."

"Kate read it?"

"Yes. I dropped it by accident and she picked it up. You know how curious kids are."

"And her reaction?"

"She thought it was hilarious."

"Typical," Sam laughed. When he laughed it was more like a chuckle; he raised his shoulders and his heavy head seemed to want to disappear between them like a turtle in its shell. "Typical."

"I told her not to mention it to anyone, not even to Kitty."

"You certainly are an ass," Sam told him, taking a swig. "What's the kid to do if she has a delayed reaction? Wait till she can talk to you about it and find out that you take it seriously. It'll put the holy bejesus into her. And eventually you're going to have to tell Kitty."

"And have her worry too?"

"Who doesn't have worries today?"

"But I don't want Kitty to have to worry about anything like this."

"Kate's the one who should be spared worry. At her age ..."

"Kate knows a lot more about what life is like today than girls her age did in our day. She recognizes danger, whereas Kitty hates to recognize anything wrong."

"Time she learned." Sam picked up the letter again. "A nut. A real nut," he said, shaking his head. "I tend to agree with you. I can't see a woman writing anything like this." He looked up, grinned. "Guess we have a glorified opinion of the fair sex. Want my advice?"

"Why do you think I showed you the letter? But you know what really worries me? There's been plenty of mail, a lot of it friendly, congratulating me on having survived, some of it hate mail, which the line tells me is normal, but all of it ... Sam, all of it went to the line. This damn thing," he brought his fist down hard on the letter, "was addressed to me here, and whoever wrote it knows I have a daughter called Kate."

Sam was silent for a moment. Then he said, "You have a point there." He hesitated. "Take it to the F.B.I."

"I've already notified them. I've got an appointment with them for tomorrow morning."

4

Shortly after Sam had left, Kitty drove in. She honked three times, three short, sharp honks, their signal to let the other know he had arrived. There was Zero's joyous barking and Kate's excited voice and another, gentle voice. Anna Barlov.

At first it had bothered Kent that Kitty seemed to consider it her duty to suddenly see so much of Anna. 'I can't stand the sight of her on crutches," he had said. But Kitty had smiled. "She'd be on your mind anyhow, wouldn't she? It's better to face her and let nothing disturb our friendship." It had surprised him because there had been a time when Kitty had been jealous of Anna.

He got up and looked through the window. She was the most fascinating girl he'd ever known, graceful as a birch tree, with a skin as white as birch bark and huge eyes, so dominant that her narrow lovely features seemed to disappear when she looked at you. The small aristocratic nose, the high cheekbones, the wide, generous mouth. Black eyes like pools in a dense forest, flecked with gold.

In some strange way it had never troubled him to think of the people who had died in the crash; what their death meant to their families and friends, yes, but not their death. You were born to die, and when your number was up, well, that was it. But what had made an impact on him were the survivors who had been hurt badly, and most of all Anna. But her tragedy had made no difference to their relationship. Gazing down at her Kent remembered the moment when Nancy, one of the stewardesses, had come to the cockpit to complain about the behavior of the passengers, quite a few of whom had come on board drunk, and she had added, "By the way, your friend the dancer is on board, but she's behaving."

Yes, Anna Barlov, returning from a concert appearance in Louisville, had been on the plane. He had left the cockpit for a moment to say hello. She had introduced him to the man sitting beside her, Gilbert Gordon, whose estate lay some miles away from where Kent lived. He hadn't known that Anna knew Gordon. Or perhaps they had just met on the plane by chance? "And that's my father," she had told him, pointing to a small man sitting in front of them. "He's going to spend a few weeks with me."

Kent knew from the papers that Anna's appearance with the American Concert Company had been a great success and that she was lined up for further engagements, and he had congratulated her. And now? He shuddered. The crash had robbed her of her right leg. It had had to be amputated below the knee.

"Come on down, Thomas," she called, as she saw his face at the window. "Join us. Kate says the water's warm enough for a swim, so I brought my bathing suit."

Whatever tears she may have shed, whatever rage she may have felt toward the fate that had ruined her career, she had never talked about it to him.

Kitty was in the kitchen, fixing coffee and putting cakes and cookies on a plate while the water was boiling. She too was beautiful, though in a more conventional way. A typical American beauty with wide-set, pale blue eyes, like Kate's, and when she smiled, dimples where you didn't expect them. She had been an airplane hostess until a passenger had noticed her and talked her into becoming a model, in the course of which she had become quite well known. "Go on out," she told Kent, "and send Kate in to help with the trays. Isn't it a lovely day? And the fridge works like a charm. Kate told me Sam looked after it. Thank God for him. Saved us fifteen bucks."

"At least," said Kent, and for a second laid one hand on her pumpkin colored hair, then he went out to the pool.

Again Kate had locked Zero up. Anna was one of his favorites and he might possibly jump up at her and make her lose her precarious balance. His yelps of frustration could be heard annoyingly from the garage. Anna was already in the pool; Kate swimming beside her as if she had been appointed her lifeguard.

"Wonderful news!" Anna called out to him. "They've finally fitted me with one of those beautiful contraptions to strap on. In no time I'll be off crutches, able to walk, do almost anything."

"Except dance," said the man whom Kent hadn't been able to see from the window, Anna's father, Stanislav Barlov, who — how ironically, how tragically, thought Kent — had escaped the crash unharmed. He had searched like a maniac among the bodies scattered on the snow-covered ground for his daughter, after which he had made a nuisance of himself to the doctors and nurses at the hospital.

Barlov looked older than his sixty odd years. You got the impression that his face had the consistency of a rubber ball on which the imprint of a finger might leave a dent. Incredible that his squat, ugly body should have been able to produce such a beautiful creature.

"Oh, I don't know," Anna answered, hanging onto the rim of the pool and lifting her face for Thomas to blow him a kiss. "Maybe somebody will dream up a ballet in which a lovely princess loses one of her legs but her lover doesn't care. A real fairy tale. The first part would, of course, have to be danced by somebody else, but I could do the second."

She hadn't always spoken so lightly, nor so hopefully, Kate thought. There had been outbreaks of despair. "Why me?" Only when her father had been utterly unable to control himself in her presence and instead of calming her, had ranted and raved against the Lord and even more violently against Kent, had she found the discipline within herself to put a stop to her hysteria as she tried to calm him.

Her radiant smile apparently infuriated her father. "A fool," he said. "That's what she is. Filled with illusions. I've lost all mine. Whatever dreams I had for her went down with your plane."

Though he spoke excellent English, he still had a heavy

Polish accent. "What do you think, Mr. Kent," he asked now. "When will the line settle with us?"

It might take years, Kent knew, but didn't say so.

"Our lawyer is trying to line up all the people who have a claim so that we can get together . . ."

"A good idea," said Kent.

Kitty's voice, from the house, "Kate! For God's sake where are you?"

"Hop out," said Anna. "I'm perfectly all right."

Kent stared at Anna's leg where the amputation had finally healed. So did Barlov. "God is not just," he said. "Why couldn't it have been me? She had everything to look forward to, while to me . . . what difference would it have made to me?"

"Coffee or a drink?" asked Kate, appearing with a tray.

"A vodka," said Anna, refusing any help as she climbed up the ladder, raising herself mainly by the arms. "That is, if you'll join me, Thomas. The water was colder than I thought."

"I want tea," said Barlov. "With jam. No sugar."

"Tea, Mom," Kate called out, and Kent said more sharply than he had intended, "You go make it."

Anna tottered slightly as she reached for her bathrobe. Kate, as if she had eyes in the back of her head, ran to the pool.

"Clumsy, aren't I?" said Anna. "Well, I'll just have to exercise more. They told me at the hospital what to do."

"You look exhausted," her father told her. "You should never have got into that damned water. And now you'll catch cold. Let's get home as quickly as we can. We shouldn't have come in the first place. Mrs. Kent will have to drive us home right away."

"You mind, Kit?" Anna asked, as Kitty set down the tray with coffee and cakes. "If you're too busy, maybe Kate would call a taxi."

"Too expensive," said Barlov.

"Charge it to me," said Kent.

"Oh, for God's sake," cried Anna, "you've been kind enough as it is."

"Kind?" Mr. Barlov sneered. "Kind is the least he

28

could be after what he did to you. He's just trying to redeem himself."

Heavens, thought Kitty, he's going to have another one of his hysterical outbursts, and it will have an affect on Kent. "Cool it," Kate wanted to yell, but knew that trying to interfere would only infuriate Anna's father. Anna, though, spoke up softly, in Polish. "*Drogi Tatus.* Won't you understand that it wasn't Mr. Kent's fault but..."

"I'm sick of your making excuses for him." Mr. Barlov's face was red with fury. "He simply isn't a good pilot or he would have prevented the crash. He should be fired, but if I'm correct, he's going back to flying, endangering other people's lives and happiness."

For a fleeting moment Kent, watching the older man's face, wondered if Barlov mightn't have written the letter. "Redeem," he thought. The word had stood out on the blue watermarked paper.

"He..." Barlov began again, but Anna said sharply, "*Ciska,*" and as bidden, Barlov shut up. Turning to Kate, Anna asked her to please call a taxi.

"But I'll gladly drive you home," said Kitty.

"*Nie,*" Anna told her. "I'd rather have a taxi." Obviously she wanted to spare Kitty her father's ravings.

There was a definite sense of relief when the taxi had finally driven off with Anna and her distraught father. Kitty turned to Kent. He was frowning, his face was tense. "Don't let him upset you," she said. "Poor guy. He can't help it."

Kent stared at the sky, so wide and blue above him, with just a few clouds sailing across it, like boats racing across an as yet uncharted sea. "I understand him, his fury, his frustration, his feeling of helplessness. I don't know how I would behave if what happened to Anna should happen to Kate."

Kitty could feel the blood draining from her face. With great effort she pulled herself together, managed to laugh. "What's come over you, Kent? Come on, let's go for a walk. Or are you too tired?"

"I walked a mile today," Kent lied. "I'd rather stay and rest, if you don't mind."

29

"Kate made you any lunch yet?"

Kate looked stricken. She'd had a hamburger at McDonald's on her way home.

"I wasn't hungry," said Kent.

"Then Kate can mow the lawn while I put in some plants. I bought some beautiful ones at a roadstand. Not just flowers, but tomatoes and all sorts of herbs."

"We should put in potatoes," said Kate. "Sam says they're going to go sky high. Anything you want me to do for you today, Thomas?"

"Just let your mother and me sit quietly for a while. Alone."

Kate disappeared into the garage to let Zero out. Then she went to the garden shed and changed into jeans. She thought of phoning Jerry. He could help with the lawn, then thought better of it. Too much commotion when Thomas looked so peaked. She went back to the garage and busied herself with the mower, an old model. They should get the kind you could ride on. Maybe if she could solve one of those puzzles in the paper that promised the most spectacular prizes, she could win one.

Kent, sitting beside Kitty, was tempted to pull out the letter and show it to her. He resisted the impulse and sat quietly, holding her hand. "You look lovely," he told her, "with your hair done up high like that. But actually I prefer it when it just hangs naturally around your face."

"That's the wrong thing to say to a woman who has just spent two hours in the beauty parlor making herself attractive for her guy."

"I always say the wrong thing, don't I?"

"Not always."

"I love you."

"That's better."

"But I don't exactly know why."

"If you did, it wouldn't be love. Just a kind of evaluation."

"I'll buy that. One doesn't love because, but in spite of."

"In spite of what?"

"In spite of the fact that you go out quite a lot by yourself."

"Who told me not to stay at home all the time with ... you said it ... a cripple?"

"You went dancing with Sam the other night, or maybe not dancing but just for a drink at Parks."

"Sometimes I feel sorry for Sam," Kitty told him. "He doesn't have a soul. Not that he seems to mind."

"He was in love with you once, wasn't he?"

"Oh, that ... that's ancient history. Too far back for either of us to remember. And he never meant a thing to me, certainly not that way. Sam's an old shoe, and he knows it. Big brother for a few years and I was the girl next door. How corny can you get? And there's nobody else. Never has been. Kent, you got yourself a virgin. Do you know what that means in this day and age? And a faithful wife. I'll stay home with you night after night if you want me to. All you have to do is say so."

"That's what I wanted to hear."

Kitty giggled. "If you aren't the stupidest guy ..."

Kent leaned over and kissed her.

5

STILL, THAT NIGHT Kent had one of the nightmares that so
mercifully hadn't disturbed his sleep for weeks. Until the
crash, the doors between their bedrooms had been closed.
It had been Kitty who had insisted on this privacy. At
the beginning of their marriage he had resented it and
Kitty hadn't been able to understand that he didn't feel
the need to be alone at times. "I want to feel you near
me," he said. "To link my big toe in yours, to put my
head on your shoulder."

"But I'm not locking my door," she said told him. "It
opens quite easily. It's not difficult to lift a cover, even if
I'm asleep. Maybe I'll wake up, maybe I won't. All I
want is not to be taken for granted. And I don't want
to take you for granted. In a way of course, yes, when
there's a need. Always when there's a need. But I must be
permitted to be alone sometimes." But since the crash, the
door between his and her room had stood wide open, so
had the door to Kate's bedroom, on the opposite side,
both ready to come to his help should he need to get out
of bed or want something that wasn't within his reach.
Kitty had never needed to be told what he wanted; often,
when it had been nothing more than the desire to feel her
beside him, she had sat at the edge of his bed, rubbed
his good foot or his head until he had fallen asleep. It had
been Kate, though, who had known best how to deal with
the nightmares. It had been her idea to bring up the
stereo from the living room downstairs and place the
record holder next to his night table. "I should have
thought of it," Kitty had said. "I'm stupid." "You're not
stupid," he had told her. "Not exactly," she had said, "but
I have no imagination. Thank God. I can't imagine what
life would be like without you, or if something should

happen to Kate." But that night he sat up in bed, scream-
ing.

His screams brought Kitty and Kate running into his
room. But they were not the outcries of fear and anguish
they had heard during the first weeks, after his release
from the hospital, nor was his face white and drawn, but
alive with rage. Zero was licking his hand.

He pushed the dog away with a gesture that was almost
brutal. "But I've just told you what happened."

"No, you haven't," said Kitty. "What happened?"

Kent had never talked to her about the crash. All he
had said that night at the hospital, where she had sat,
waiting for him to come around, was that it had been one
of those days when he had awakened with the feeling that
something would go wrong. Now he was staring at her as
if she were a stranger, unseeingly, then he fell back on his
pillows, his eyes closed, breathing heavily. They waited.
"He's fallen asleep," whispered Kate, but Kitty shook her
head. She touched Kent's hand gently. "Kent. What
happened?"

He didn't answer. In an effort to make him go on
speaking, Kitty said, "Henderson told us that the crew had
been unable to get the landing gear down, and had been
successful only after repeated attempts."

Henderson, Kent's co-pilot, who had escaped mirac-
ulously unharmed, had spent what was left of the night
of the crash at their house, but he hadn't talked about the
crash either, possibly because he'd gotten drunk, so drunk
that Kitty had had to call his wife in Winsted to tell her
that her husband was all right, just shaken up a bit and
therefore not coming home until next morning.

Her words didn't seem to reach Kent, but then, to her
surprise, he began to talk again, in a far away voice, not
really to them but rather as if he were again addressing
the NTSB.

"I don't deny that I was nervous that day, and apprehensive. There are days when I wake with the feeling that
things will go wrong. But that's always made me more
careful, more alert. It hasn't frightened or disturbed me,
nor upset me. But when I read in the maintenance log for

aircraft number 715, the equipment assigned to flight 234, and noted that the crew that had brought the plane from Louisville had written up a potentially serious problem, my apprehension deepened. They had been unable to get the landing gear of the Boeing 727 down and been successful only after repeated attempts. For some reason the wheels had got stuck in the 'up' position. I knew that other airlines had experienced similar problems with this type of aircraft and had failed to find a conclusive cause for the landing gear's malfunction, which did nothing to relieve my nervousness. Yet the maintenance department in Louisville had signed off the log, stating 'up-lock cleaned and greased', the hydraulic system was functioning normally — I therefore decided to accept the aircraft and fly it to Kennedy where they had better facilities for testing it."

Once more he stopped speaking. Neither Kitty nor Kate dared to urge him to go on. There was something about him that seemed to negate their presence and Kitty sensed that this was just what was making it possible for him to talk about it, and that it was absolutely essential that he do so. His pale, pained face was almost unbearable to watch, but Kitty forced herself to keep her eyes on his. "Go on," she said.

"After filing the flight plan and checking the already bad weather conditions, I found that they had deteriorated in the New York area, making it doubtful that flight 234 could even get into Kennedy. The bad weather, compounded with the gear problem, made me feel even more uneasy. I directed the flight operation man to load extra fuel, anticipating holding delays, not only due to the weather but also because of an annoying Air Traffic Controller's slowdown that had complicated east coast flight operations for the past two weeks. Fuel shortages and costs had made my request for more fuel a point of contention between me and the dispatcher, and the haggling over that increased my state of agitation. I calmed down somewhat after I got flight 234 into the air. The departure was on time and uneventful."

Not so uneventful, thought Kitty. Nancy Freed, one of the stewardesses who had survived the crash had come

34

to visit Kent in the hospital, had talked about the obstreperous behavior of the passengers on Kent's flight. Some had missed an earlier connection and been delayed in Louisville for more than two hours, most of which they seemed to have spent in the bar. They had been unruly, and she and Gertrude, the other stewardess, had had a difficult time getting them to sit down for the approach into the New York area. Severe turbulence was expected, but many of them had simply ignored the "Fasten seat belts" sign. Again and again she and Gertrude had appeared in the cockpit with distracting complaints about them.

Kent sat up, his voice became shriller. "After receiving weather reports from an en route company station in Baltimore, I learned that Kennedy was experiencing high winds, with gusts up to sixty knots, heavy snow showers mixed with freezing rain, and poor braking conditions on the runways. Although the controllers seemed to be doing a good job, the severe weather had forced holding delays up to two hours. I was now faced," Kent's voice was normal again, but unusually slow, "with the decision to divert my flight to Washington, which was my alternate and where the weather was less severe, or take my already delayed passengers to their destination, Kennedy airport. But at Kennedy," now Kent was staring at Kate, just as he had stared at Kitty before, unseeingly, "they could check the gear problem more thoroughly. I knew landing there would be difficult, but I had made landings under worse conditions. With the landing gear problem bugging me, I decided to remain on course for Kennedy. Yes, I made that decision."

Kitty glanced at Kate. The girl's eyes were fixed unblinkingly on her father. "As I had expected," he went on, "the flight was put in a holding pattern as soon as I approached the New York area. Air Traffic directed flight 234 to hold over Atlantic City at 27,000 feet. I circled for almost two hours, occasionally cleared down to lower altitudes. I'd been wise to push for extra fuel. But circling at lower and lower altitudes consumed much of my reserve fuel.

"The mental and physical strain of guiding the plane in

35

the severe weather and turbulence was exhausting, even with the help of my auto-pilot. And my co-pilot, Henderson, was of little help. Miserable flight conditions like that demand the skill of an ace, and Henderson didn't put in more than an average performance."

Henderson, thought Kitty. She had never liked him.

"The approach controller," Kent was saying, "guided the plane down expertly, and everything seemed to be proceeding smoothly until it came time to lower the landing gear. To my horror," now his voice was quiet and controlled again, "it wouldn't come down. I informed approach control that I was proceeding with a missed approach. Approach control directed me by radar to an emergency holding pattern to give me time to straighten out my problem. I felt I would probably have to consider an emergency landing since the gear had failed to function properly. Better weather conditions would have made the job much easier. But by now the entire east coast from Norfolk to Canada was closed in by the freak winter storm, making my alternate airport, Washington, just as hazardous as Kennedy."

Kent's voice rose suddenly. "I was running short of fuel because of the extended delay. The problem was becoming more critical. Each passing minute circling over the holding point meant less fuel. The engineer consulted the aircraft manuals to see if there was any possible way to correct the landing gear malfunction. The flight was receiving assistance from the company maintenance engineers at JFK. They were consulting manuals, questioning computer read-outs, and trying by every means available to solve the gear problem in the short time allotted to them. Within an hour I knew I had no choice but to make an emergency landing. I'd made several of them, and wasn't afraid of this one, although I wished I could have relied more on Henderson. I informed approach control that I was declaring an emergency and would land in forty-five minutes."

An emergency landing, as Kitty knew well from her days as an airline stewardess, could tie up the active runways for as much as four to five hours, if crews were required to clear away a disabled aircraft. And certainly there must have been many more incoming flights in holding patterns on that evening, also dangerously low on fuel. Why in the world had she ever married a pilot?

Kent was staring at her, his eyes void of all expression. "Air Traffic Control couldn't order emergency crews to spread a cushion of spark-arresting foam on 31 L. They couldn't risk having other waiting planes drop into the sea from fuel starvation, since all other airports in the area were now closed."

"I don't understand," whispered Kate. "Why not?"

Kitty shook her head, commanding silence. All that mattered was that Kent should get everything out. Kent, though, replied. "Couldn't afford it because of a closed runway. Their only recourse was to direct flight 234 to runway 4 R, which would relieve the problem of the congested skies, but would force me to land in a ninety degree crosswind. I directed the flight attendants to prepare the passengers for an emergency landing. While Air Traffic Control directed other traffic away from the area, I prepared for the landing."

Once more his face showed the tenseness and agony he must have felt then. "Wind and driving snow continued unabated, impeding those who were trying to spread the foam. It wouldn't stick to the icy landing area and the wind slapped it back at the workers. The severe gusts and low visibility made my approach almost impossible. I brought my plane down to the minimum altitude but found I was coming in too far to one side of the runway. I was forced to make another approach and pulled up to make a go-around.

"When I brought the stricken plane down," Kent smiled unexpectedly, an almost contented smile, as if he were still in the cockpit, believing in his ability and luck, "I was lined up perfectly for a touchdown on the sparsely foamed runway, and felt almost certain that I stood a reasonable chance of a successful belly landing."

He paused. "And then?" asked Kate, ignoring her mother's signs to keep quiet.

"And then," said Kent, still smiling with satisfaction,

37

"the plane touched down at exactly the right spot, at exactly the right speed. I shut down the engines immediately to prevent fire." The smile left his face. He closed his eyes and his voice became a scream that made Kitty shudder and Zero bark furiously.

"The wind, that terrible crosswind caught the plane's high vertical stabilizer and began to weathercock it into the wind. It caused my plane to veer sharply off the runway. It skidded across the snowy, frozen ground. It was forced directly into the tank farm, the underground fuel storage facility with its maze of pipes and concrete walls."

The tears spilled down from his open eyes. "The fuselage hit a drainage ditch, causing it to whip around as it made contact with the tank farm. It cracked in half. The entire wing and the tail section exploded, killing all those inside. Most of those in front escaped serious injury, but . . ."

He was silent. He fell back on his pillows as if released from the witness stand, his face serene. Soon, by his steady breathing, they could tell that he had fallen asleep.

6

A WHITE FOUR-POSTER bed with a lacy cover over the thin curved slats that spanned it. Blue and white gingham sheets. A toy panda with a long red tongue hanging down over its furry white chin. Kate was hugging it. On her night table, a box with the stones she collected, a boyish trait, thought Kitty. Onyx, lapis lazuli, chrysoprase, an almost hand-size rock of purple amethyst crystal. Already one year old and barely able to walk, Kate had been fascinated by stones. If nobody was watching, she'd put any pebble in her mouth for safekeeping.

Kitty sat down on the rocking chair, an antique one on which Kent had worked on and off for weeks, taking off the horrible paint to bring back the glory of honey-colored maple. She rocked gently. "I wonder what brought it on. Today. I thought he'd gotten over it."

Kate put the panda on top of her head and stroked the animal's feet. For years she had pleaded with her parents to give her a real live panda for a Christmas present. Hard to get and terribly expensive. Instead they had put in the swimming pool.

"He was alone all morning," Kitty mused. "Maybe I shouldn't have gone to the hairdresser, but taken Thomas with me to town."

She rarely called him by his first name, mostly Kent. "Or perhaps it was Anna. I mean in the pool, with her leg exposed. Maybe we shouldn't have proposed a swim, but she was so eager when you told her you'd been in for a dip in the morning. Or maybe that awful father of hers, the things he said."

"It wasn't because he was alone," said Kate, "and it wasn't Anna or anything that was said. It was the letter he got this morning."

There it was, slipped out in spite of her intention not to mention it. She had broken a promise, a promise she had given to, of all persons, Thomas. Even by the dim light of the nightlight that was always kept burning in her and Kitty's room since the crash, Kitty could see the consternation on Kate's face. "What letter?" she asked softly.

Kate took the panda off her head and held it in front of her face. She didn't answer.

"I asked you a question," said Kitty.

"I didn't hear you," said Kate.

"I asked you — what letter? You mentioned a letter Kent got and I want to know what kind of a letter it was."

"He didn't show it to me."

"Then what makes you think that it upset him? You read it, didn't you?"

"I did," said Kate. "He dropped it and I picked it up, and I couldn't help reading it."

"And your father knows you did?"

"Mom." Kate threw the panda aside and sat up straight. "I gave him my word of honor not to say anything about it to anyone."

"But you did," said Kitty, her voice unusually stern. "It's difficult to keep a secret, but once you've let it out, you have to follow up."

"Don't make me break a promise."

"I don't want to, actually," Kitty told her, reaching out for the small, cold trembling hand. "But if it had such an effect on him, I must know. I worry about him just as much as you do, and I love him just as much as you love him."

"Do you?"

For a second Kitty was startled. Had Kate put the question to her to stall her, or did it have a deeper meaning?

"I do," she said. "Why do you ask?"

"You spend such a lot of time away from each other, and neither of you seems to mind. If I were married . . ."

"You'll find out that the closer you are, the more secure

40

you feel. Then separation doesn't mean much. Now tell me about the letter."

"Not unless you promise me not to tell him I told you."

Suddenly Kitty was angry; angry at Kate, angry at herself, that a mother's authority seemed to have no impact. Although they had never been permissive, they had always respected Kate as an individual. And now she was forced to bargain with her. Anyhow, this was the age when children usually came to resent their parents' authority, when a girl Kate's age was beginning to feel like a young woman. Kate and she had been at odds for more than a year.

"I want to know what was in that letter without your making any conditions."

Kate squirmed. She said, "Mom, if I don't want to tell you, it's because Thomas and I love you," and knew at once that it was the wrong thing.

"You can only love a person if you truly respect him, and apparently neither Kent nor you think I'm grown up enough to share your worries."

Kate fell into the trap. "We adore you," she said, "and you know it. It was a silly letter, the letter of a madman. Something about that he had no right to enjoy life when he was guilty of having caused so much misery, and he should kill himself to make up for the crash." She forced herself to laugh. "Something, ain't it? Just plain crazy."

"Or?" asked Kitty.

"Or what?"

"If you threaten someone, you usually give an alternative."

There was a long silence. "Or?" repeated Kitty.

"Or . . . or he would take his revenge on me."

Kitty said nothing, but Kate noticed that her mother had stopped rocking. "Don't tell Thomas I told you."

"Where is the letter?"

"He put it in his pocket."

Kitty stared at Kate as if she had never seen her child before. Her child. The only child she would ever have after that damned hysterectomy. She got up quickly. Kate could hear her move around Kent's bedroom, then go across the hall to his study. After a few quiet moments she came back into Kate's room and sat down in the rocker again. "I've read it," she said. "You're right. The letter of a maniac. And don't worry. I won't tell your father. But does it frighten you?"

"Frighten me?" This time Kate's laugh didn't sound forced. "But what about you? You look awfully serious suddenly."

"It doesn't frighten me in the least," Kitty told her. "What about a snack? I don't know what makes me hungry all of a sudden. An omelet would be just the right thing."

"They never come out the way I want them to," said Kate. "They always stick to the pan."

Kitty laughed. "I'll show you how to do it."

7

THOMAS KENT SLEPT, so did Zero, curled up at the foot of the bed. Kate slept fitfully, wakened periodically by a terrible feeling of guilt for having broken her promise to her father. Kitty Kent didn't sleep at all.

She was profoundly disturbed. There had been some hate mail to the airline, where they had assured her this was quite normal. Some people had to vent their grief or anger over their loss on whomever they thought responsible, and a scapegoat could always be found. None of the hate mail, however, had directed a menace against Kate. But now? Why was she so terribly upset? Was it because she felt that somehow Kent could take care of himself whereas her daughter was much more vulnerable? Or was it because her love for Kate, her need for her child, was deeper than her love or need for Kent?

Kitty got up from her bed and went into Kent's study. She sat down in front of the long, narrow table. She touched the globe that stood at one end, stared at the map facing her, nailed to the wall, with all the routes he flew or had flown, pinpointed with different colored pins. Miami — Albany. New York — Sao Paulo. Washington — Albany. Boston — Chicago. New York — London. And other places overseas. There was a small tray next to the globe, an ice container — Kate's duty was to keep it filled. A bottle of scotch, Cutty Sark. A glass. She poured herself a stiff drink. She took a cigarette from a half-filled pack. Why did Kent have to smoke such heavy cigarettes? And lighted it. Drinking and smoking, she sat there asking herself the question, "What now?"

Why didn't Kent want her to know about the insane letter? Was he taking it seriously? She almost got up to go into his room to ask him, then sat down again. Wake him from his exhausted sleep? No. Not now. At this point he couldn't be expected to make sense.

All the intrusions of an imagination she had always claimed she didn't have now took possession of her. What if Kent committed suicide to meet the demands that would save Kate? What if he didn't, and as a consequence, Kate would be hurt? Kent was not a man to kill himself. She had never known a man with such a zest for life. But he loved Kate just as much as she did. If not more. What if he decided that a young life was worth saving above everything else? But then, what would it do to Kate to lose her father? What if he decided — as he apparently had done, if only not to frighten Kate — to ignore the threat, as he had always ignored danger? And in consequence...

She didn't dare to ask herself whose death would affect her more. She tried to pull herself together. Dismiss it, she told herself, and would have dismissed it if Kent hadn't made Kate promise not to mention it to her. Was he taking it seriously? I love you, Kitty thought. You have no idea how deeply. You've taught me how to enjoy life. Without you, Kent... but without Kate? If anything happened to Kate, it would break Kent. Oh, dear Lord in heaven...

"Shit!" Kitty said aloud. "I'm being hysterical. I'd better stop it. I'd better think what to do about this situation." She thought of phoning Maximillian Forster. Perhaps he would have some advice. She smiled fleetingly as she thought of the man who once had played such a decisive part in her life. Now they saw each other only occasionally. She looked at her watch and dropped the idea of contacting him. It was too late to ring him. He would either be out or asleep.

She poured herself another drink, shaking her head. She hardly ever smoked, she never touched hard liquor, perhaps because her father had been high the night he'd run his old jalopy into a tree, killing them both, him and her mother. Twelve years old at the time, she had reacted with fury, taking her parents' death as a wilfull abandonment, before the realization of loss had set in. The follow-

44

ing years had, in many ways, been agony. An aunt, twice removed, had taken her in, a woman who had always wanted a daughter but had given birth to three sons instead. She had been a good enough mother, but the boys had resented her and made life hell. If it hadn't been for Sam, living next door, she wouldn't have had a confidant, or rather, a protector. Both of them had wanted to go to college. He couldn't because there wasn't enough money, and her aunt had been old-fashioned enough to believe that girls didn't need to study but should go to business school and become secretaries and one day marry. Confiding in Sam, she had told him she wanted to see the world and together they had cooked up the idea of her becoming an airplane hostess. With all her pocket-money saved up, she had written in for Berlitz courses and had studied like mad, hidden in the tree-house he had built for her, where she was safe from her cousins, using Sam to listen endlessly to new vocabularies, writing out exams that came by mail, general delivery. Except for a while, when he had thought he was in love with her. After that silly period, they had lost track of each other for many years.

Impulsively Kitty picked up the receiver and called Sam Slew. She had to let the phone ring several times before he answered, his voice heavy with sleep. "Who in the world . . . it's half past two!"

"It's me. Kitty."

"Kitty?" He coughed, then asked, "What do you want?"

"Sorry to disturb you, but it's important."

"What's important?"

"You've got to promise not to mention what I'm going to tell you to a soul."

"For Christ's sake, Kitty, get on with it!"

"It's just by chance that I found out . . ." Kitty had trouble phrasing her words, something that rarely happened. "Kent got a letter today . . ."

"I know about that shitty letter," Sam told her. Without giving her time to ask how come, he went on quickly. "Tom told me about it. He let me read it. Don't give it a thought. A crank's letter."

45

"All right. So why didn't Kent tell me about it?"

"For God's sake, Kit, what man would want his woman to worry . . ."

"But is *he* worrying about it?" Kitty crushed her cigarette.

"No man in his right mind takes anything like that seriously," said Sam. "I get anonymous letters all the time because I won't employ union workers. You throw them away. Nobody pays attention to that kind of crap. Go to sleep, Kit. Forget it. See ya . . ."

"Sam . . ." But he had hung up.

Kitty put down the receiver. She got up, took the empty glass and the dirty ashtray down to the kitchen and cleaned them quite automatically. Anything dirty was offensive to her. And she had taught Kate to wash, dry and put away any extra dishes so that the kitchen always looked almost unused. She took the garbage pail and put it out, then went to put on the light in the driveway, something she would not ordinarily have done. She whistled for Zero to come down, but Zero didn't react. She went upstairs and turned on the light in the hall. She looked in on Kate. Kate was fast asleep, her head resting on the panda's stomach. Her lashes threw shadows on her smooth cheeks. Kitty felt like bending over to kiss her, but restrained herself. Whom did she need more? Love more? Kent? Kate?

She walked into Kent's room. Zero lifted his head in recognition, then put it back between his paws. Kitty Kent stood for a long time looking down at her husband, the man she loved, who lay straight on his back without stirring, eyes closed, an almost peaceful expression on his pale face. She had chosen him. Reversing the conventions that had still been more or less the rule at the time, she had been the impetus and had told him she wanted to live with him. Kent had reacted old-fashionedly. If he lived with a woman, he had declared, he would feel compelled to marry her. And he didn't think a man should marry before thirty, by which time he should know what he really wanted.

"But I don't want to get married," Kitty had said.

"And if you became pregnant, would you abort?"

"Never."

"Because you think it's a sin?"

"Not at all. Because I want a child."

"Without a father?"

"I'm quite able to take care of my child without your or anybody's help."

Liberated, they'd call it now, but she'd been only twenty then and always thought of herself as totally independent, ever since the death of her parents.

"Oh Kent, my poor Kent," she thought. "In what a ghastly position you have been put." She felt like throwing off her robe and lying down beside him, just to feel him, warm him, warm herself. A moment later her tenderness changed to anger. He had shut her out, away from his problem.

As if he felt her presence, he opened his eyes, saw her, and with one sleepy, clumsy gesture, lifted the covers. Kitty slipped next to him, her head on his shoulder, careful not to touch his bad foot. Zero growled, annoyed for a second, then stopped as her feet stroked him gently. The house was quiet, yet filled for her with a terror that seemed to ooze slowly from its very base to the slate on the roof, some of which had been replaced only last week. Exactly the atmosphere the writer of the letter had intended.

8

AT A LITTLE after seven, Kitty was awakened from a
heavy sleep by the sound of Kent moving around in his
room. He had made a point during the last weeks of
dressing himself without her help, but he never got up this
early, not until Kate had left for school. Wide awake
suddenly, she walked into his room. He was fully dressed,
knotting a tie. A tie in the country?

"What are you doing up so early?"

He didn't turn to face her. "You were fast asleep. I'm
sorry I woke you up. I have to make the eight fifteen to
New York. I thought I'd drop Kate off at school."

"But why do you have to go to New York?"

He didn't answer but went on dressing hurriedly. "Kent,
I must talk to you."

"Not now," he said. "When I get back."

"But I can drive you in."

"No." His answer was short, almost rude. "I've called a
taxi. Kate, are you ready?"

Kitty knew from experience that there was no way of
stopping him once he had made up his mind. Besides,
what she wanted to talk about couldn't be settled in a
hurry. "Then tell me at least when you think you'll be
back," she said, as she followed him downstairs. "I'll pick
you up."

"I'll give you a ring from New York," and he left her
standing helplessly in the hall. Kate, hurrying past her,
only had time to blow her a kiss as she tore out the door
and climbed after Kent into the waiting car. Kitty sat
down on the bottom step and began to cry.

The day seemed endless. In the morning she tried to busy
herself with all sorts of things. She shopped. For moments
she could dismiss the fears that were nagging at her, then

again she fell prey to them. Slowly the day dragged on. Around noon the phone rang. She rushed to pick it up, but it wasn't Kent. At two p.m., the same thing. He didn't call as he had promised.

He came back about six, just when she had decided to take a bath to soothe her nerves. From downstairs came Kate's jubilant voice, "Thomas, I've got to tell you ... I've ..."

"Not now," she heard him reply. "Where's your mother?"

"Up here," she called out to him. "Taking a bath."

He came into the bathroom and sat down on the stool. "You mind?"

"Watching me soak? Not at all." He looked exhausted.

For a while they didn't speak, then she asked, "Kent, what's wrong?"

"Nothing's wrong. Why?"

"You're acting strangely."

He shrugged, took his pipe and tobacco pouch out of his pocket, hesitated, looked at her, and when she nodded stuffed it expertly and lighted it. The smell of tobacco mingled with that of the pine needle oil in the bath. She waited patiently, then sat up, but feeling the warmth of the hot water leaving her shoulders and breasts, sank down again. "Kent," she said, "I know it's the letter you got yesterday."

"Did Kate tell you?"

She shook her head.

"Then who did?"

"Sam," she lied. "I met him this morning at Sears. I was looking for a stationary bicycle for you to exercise your leg when the cast's off."

"The louse," said Kent. "I thought I'd made it pretty clear to him that I didn't want you worried with it."

"That's just the point," said Kitty. "I'm a grown woman who doesn't shy away from the bitter facts of life, and paranoiacs have always been part of it. I am also your wife and the mother of our only child, and I demand the right to share whatever worries you. Naturally I'm upset, and I can tell you are, and it offends me to be left out. As

49

a matter of fact, it infuriates me that you're keeping something so crucial from me, something so crucial to all of us."

"But don't you see that I refuse to take a crank's letter seriously, and I was afraid you might."

"Then what were you doing in New York?"

"I went to the F.B.I. Sam and I agreed that it was the thing to do."

"And he told me to forget about it. What did the F.B.I. say?"

"They took the letter, gave me a Xeroxed copy, and said they'd work on it. I am to let them know at once if anything else turns up. They also thought it might be a good thing to have Kate put under surveillance."

"Yes, what about Kate? Does she know? I hope not."

"She knows." Kent knocked his pipe on the rim of the toilet. "I wish she didn't, but I dropped the damn thing and she found it, and of course read it."

"It's unforgivable that you should have been so careless as to let her find something like that."

"I agree," said Kent. "But we'd have had to tell her anyhow. That's what the F.B.I. advised me. So far she thinks it's a huge joke."

"I wonder," said Kitty. She got out of the bath. Kent tried to hold her bathrobe for her. "Careful," she said, "you'd better hold onto your crutches."

"I can walk without them beautifully," he said.

"But you're not supposed to yet. So let's be sensible."

He followed her into her bedroom. The bed was disarranged. She must have been lying on it. And there was a drink on her bedside table. She stretched out on the bed. "Got a cigarette on you?"

Kent was taken aback. She hardly ever smoked. Or drank. It got her, he thought, as he handed her his pack. He was about to stretch out beside her, but she stopped him. "I want to see the letter."

He got it, handed it to her. She read it for the second time. The effect of the Xeroxed copy was in some ways worse than the original, somehow so criminally official.

Kent stretched out beside her, lighted a cigarette for himself, since his pipe was still too hot to refill. He drew her attention to his reasons, with which the F.B.I. had agreed, for believing the writer might be someone who knew him. "And is that supposed to make me feel better?" she asked.

"It might make it easier to track him down." He turned on his side, his face close to her. "Calm down, hon, please. They're going to work on it. Try to dismiss it from your mind."

"I can't." Her voice was small, almost inaudible. "Neither can you. Kent, let's send Kate away. Holidays are starting in a few weeks. We can take her out of school ahead of time. She's top in her class. The teachers won't mind, and what she might miss she can make up in no time. You've got friends all over the world — England, Switzerland, Italy, France . . ."

'We promised to take her to Martha's Vineyard," said Kent. "She's too smart not to guess the reason for it if we take her out of school and make her go to Europe now, all by herself. She'll figure that we're giving this thing real importance, and that wouldn't be good, would it?"

He opened her bathrobe, which she had closed tight around her, and touched her breast. "Not now," said Kitty, although she had never felt a deeper need to feel him inside her.

"Kit, love, stop worrying. I assure you nothing will happen to Kate."

"How can you be so sure?"

Suddenly another fear assailed her. A fear so strong that she felt herself trembling and turned on her stomach as if to smother it. "Kent . . . you're not going to kill yourself to save Kate from harm?"

Kent broke into gales of laughter. She turned around again to face him. How much of it was sincere or put on to give her peace of mind?

"Christ Almighty, Kit, you're nuts. You're just plain nuts. Kill myself when I have so much to live for? When life is the most wonderful thing there is? Life is for the living. Yes, one day I'll die. We're born to die, but I'm not ready for death yet. Whenever I think of it, it's always in a totally impersonal way. I'd like an easy death, of course, even if it has to be a crash. And I hope it'll come on me suddenly and decisively when I'm doing something I love — digging a hole for a new tree, or on a safari — I'd never go to kill, just to watch the animals I've not seen except in a zoo. But to kill myself because a madman threatens me . . . never!"

Kitty said nothing. He stroked some hair that had fallen into her face away from her high, rounded forehead. She was frowning. For the first time in her life she was frightened. Fear ran down her back like an icy jet of water. "Kent," she said, "if we can't take Kate away . . . then at least do something for me that will make me feel a little calmer. We don't know how seriously the F.B.I. is going to take this thing. They may have hundreds of men, but they don't know us. And the writer of the letter . . . you're quite right . . . he might very well be somebody who does. Let's get Bill Ward in on this."

"Bill Ward?"

Ward was a former policeman who had set up a private detective agency in nearby Great Neck a few years ago. "Didn't he leave the force just before they were going to downgrade him? There was talk about . . ."

"I know. He may be a little on the shady side, but that doesn't seem to prevent him from being a crack detective. Sam seems to think it helps. And Ward's familiar with the whole area."

"Well, if you really think it would ease your mind, I'll see him."

Kate appeared in the doorway. "Dinner is about ready, except for the squash. I'm not sure about how to stuff it. I cut it up all right . . ."

"I'm not hungry," said Kitty. "Thank you, darling, but I'll have a snack later."

"So will I," said Kent.

"Lovely," said Kate. 'There I stand in the kitchen, burning my paws because I couldn't find the potholder, and then you tell me . . . oh, by the way, I finally got my black belt."

52

"Congratulations," said Kitty. "I never doubted you would."

"And you promised to play three games of gin with me tonight."

"Later. Perhaps."

"Later you'll tell me it's time to go to bed."

"Later," said Kent.

"I see," said Kate. "You want to be alone. Well, I'll eat all three steaks and all of the ice cream."

"Go ahead," said Kent.

Kate slammed the door. Kitty called her back. "Would you please close it softly?"

Kate closed it softly, opened it again and stuck her head in. "I think your timing is all off. I hate to eat by myself."

Kitty swung her legs off the bed. "All right. We're coming down."

"I can hold it for half an hour," said Kate.

9

BILL WARD WAS a good-looking fellow. He knew it, and
he took good care that whatever he wore enhanced his
appearance. He was by far the most elegantly dressed man
in town, even his jeans fitted him to perfection, setting off
his slender hips and small behind. Somehow he gave the
impression that he had a lot of money and because of this
had been mugged several times by thugs who didn't know
he was a detective and carried a gun. Not that he wouldn't
dress up like a nun or a tramp or whatever disguise was
necessary for the job. He rather enjoyed that part of his
profession, just as an actor might delight in slipping into
the costumes of another time and personality.

Sam came to pick up Kent shortly after dinner, to
drive him to his meeting with Ward. "Good of you to
drive me over," said Kent.

"Never mind going to Parks," said Sam.

So there they were, in Sam's big black Mercedes, the
motor of which you couldn't hear even when it was doing
ninety. But somehow Sam always got away with it. And
he was a marvelous driver. He rode whatever car he had
— and he had several, cars being one of his hobbies — as
if it were a horse and he'd been born in the saddle.

"Good idea of yours to see Ward," he told Kent. "So
what's with the F.B.I.?"

Kent repeated what he had told Kitty. "They agreed
with me that the letter might very well be from someone
who knows me. On the other hand, they said it wouldn't
be all that difficult to find out where I lived by anyone
really determined to know. They wanted to know if I had
any suspect in mind. I didn't. And that I was to contact
them if I had any leads. The usual thing."

"You have the copy of the letter with you?"

Kent nodded.

"Good."

Parks was just a few miles beyond the new shopping center, three different restaurants in one, as it had been for years. Originally it had been an old diner where truck drivers had stopped for home-cooked pea soup with plenty of pork in it and coffee that was always strong and freshly made. Then Parks had added a room with booths, and, beyond that, a place with neatly laid tables, a bar with vinyl covered chairs and a small, highly polished dance floor. The music consisted of juke boxes, sometimes all three were playing different tunes which seemed to bother nobody. It was always crowded. Behind the bar — it had taken him quite a while to get a liquor license — and the dance floor, were three bedrooms and a small lounge which Parks claimed were his living quarters. Everybody knew better, but then Parks was discreet. Parks himself was an elderly man, undistinguished looking, who had worked his way up from dishwasher to bartender, and as usual he was behind the bar, supervising the help, making sure there was enough ice in the drinks to make them look bigger. He pointed with his chin in the direction of the lounge.

"I'd like to take a bottle of rye with me," said Sam.

Parks nodded, his special nod for "coming right up", and Sam put his hand under one of Kent's crutches to steer him over the highly polished dance floor into one of the three bedrooms. In the neighborhood it was called "the queen's suite", because, contrary to the other small, simple rooms it was furnished quite elaborately, with mirrors on the ceiling and some dreadful paintings and chintzy furniture Parks had picked up at country auctions. It was also roomy enough to hold a card table with several chairs around it.

Bill Ward was sitting at the table, playing solitaire. "Three men aren't enough for poker," he said as a greeting. "Hi, Kent. Good to see you, Sam. Why are we meeting here?"

"Because it's one of your favorite hang-outs," said Sam, "and Kent wanted privacy. And he's got something there.

Your office leaks. You do something about it, keep those kid reporters out."

"I have to take a leak right now," said Ward, got up and came back to find the rye, glasses, ice and water on the card table. He was singing softly, "I want to be the only man you kiss, I want to be the only man you miss, and if you don't agree to that, take your hat for that is that." He beamed at them. "I made that up."

"Didn't know you were a songwriter," said Sam. "But Kent didn't come here to hear your little jingle."

"So what's it all about?"

Kent pulled out the letter and handed it to Ward.

"A Xerox copy. Where's the original?"

"The F.B.I. kept it."

"Zatso?"

Ward pushed his glass aside and spread the letter out carefully in front of him.

"The original," said Kent, "was written on blue, water-marked paper, printed in red block letters. They seemed to think that tiles from a scrabble set had been used."

Ward looked up at him. "It'd make it a hell of a lot easier for me if I had the original. Printed in red block letters from a scrabble game, eh? That's what they said? What about the envelope?"

"Stamped New York, N.Y. Zip 10001 pm. Date unclear. On the same type paper. Same lettering."

Ward sat back, pushed the letter away. "Millions of scrabble games around. Know anyone, Kent, who is extremely fond of blue?"

"My wife," said Kent. "And Kate. Blue's their favorite color." Because it goes so well with their hair, he thought.

Ward picked up the letter again, looked at it, flung it down. "Couldn't deduct anything from this even if I was Sherlock Holmes."

"I think it's the letter of a madman," said Kent. "Obviously only a crank could have written it."

Ward's heavy lids fluttered. "I'm not so sure. People are strange animals. I've seen so much queer behavior, even with my wife. When she finally found out that the cancer she had was terminal, do you think she cried? No. She went to New York and came home with a sable coat. Lifted it like an ordinary thief. I give you my word. She who wouldn't have taken a cup of sugar home without telling the woman from whom she'd borrowed it. I had one hell of a time hushing it up and paying for it in monthly installments. But that's what she did. She'd always wanted a sable coat, and she wasn't going to die without having had one.'

A short silence. Kent hadn't known Ward had been married.

"So you think it may be a man who's mentally sick or someone taking his revenge on life out on me?" he asked.

"Could be," said Ward. "Twenty people died, if I remember it correctly. Let's say that might affect five in each case, more or less closely. Makes a hundred. And among the survivors... ten, weren't there? Three were badly injured. Where am I supposed to begin?"

"Look," said Kent. "The letter came to my home address. All the others, most of them friendly, except for some hate mail, went to the line. That's why my wife thought I should see you. It must be somebody who knows where I live, and that I have a daughter named Kate. I can let you have all the data I have on those who died, and on the survivors.'

"Anna Barlov's father," said Sam. "He certainly could be counted as a suspect. He's behaved like a maniac ever since his daughter was crippled. She was a dancer, you know. The threat on Kent's daughter..."

Ward had started to sing again, low voice, more a hum, "I want to be the only man you kiss, I want to be the only man you miss..." Kent interrupted him. "Ward," he said, "I'm worried. My daughter means a lot to me."

"Don't tell me you're planning to commit suicide to save her?"

"If I was, I wouldn't be sitting here asking for your help." Kent couldn't keep the anger out of his voice.

Bill Ward touched one of the crutches leaning against the card table. "A broken hip can cause trauma."

"It can." Kent reddened slightly. "And it did. But I got over it."

"Come on, Ward," said Sam. "Quit the psychology. Will you take the case or won't you?"

"Take your hat and that is that..." Ward was off again.

"For God's sake, man," said Sam. "Can't you be serious for a moment?"

"I'm thinking," said Bill Ward. "And when I'm thinking I do silly things, like making up songs or playing the big Napoleon." He shuffled his deck of cards. "Thirteen cards in four rows. Aces up front. You build from ace to king. If you get a free space after a king, it's a dead spot. Watch."

He laid the cards out. When he had laid down three of the four lines, he shoved the cards together again.

"So what do you advise me to do?"

"I want to be the only man you kiss..." Ward began his song again and Kent brought his fist down so hard on the table the liquor in their glasses spilled over. "I didn't come here to hear you sing an idiotic ditty."

Bill Ward chose to ignore Kent's fury. "All right," he said, casually. "We keep it to ourselves. You don't want it spread all over the papers: Thomas Kent's daughter threatened unless he commits suicide." He was silent for a moment, then he said, "Okay. I'll take the case. You don't have to come up with any advance payment, but I'm going to charge you plenty."

"What's plenty?" asked Kent.

"A thousand a month."

"That's pretty high."

"That's what I'm asking. Expenses not included, of course."

"I'll think it over."

"I wouldn't advise taking too long. Something might happen you wouldn't like. Once a crank's got an *idée fixe* like that," Kent wondered where he'd picked up the foreignism, "they usually follow through. Don't forget, as I just told you, twenty dead makes a hundred people suffering because of those deaths, one way or another. And that's not counting the survivors, and the thousands who've read about it and think..."

"Make it three hundred."

"Five. Absolute minimum."

"All right. Five hundred."

"Five hundred for the first month, seven-fifty for the second, if you or your Kate are still alive. And a free trip to wherever I want to go after that, for a vacation."

"And nothing if you aren't successful in the next four weeks." Kent reached for his crutches. He turned to Sam. "Come on, let's go."

"Take him home, Sam." Bill Ward was humming his little tune again, this time without the words. "He's all in, poor guy. Well, I wouldn't like to be in his position."

10

MAY IS ONE of our prettiest months. The apples are in bloom, the dogwood is ready to open, the roses are greening, and this May seems to me the prettiest one I've ever seen. Not only because everything is so early or the days are so unseasonably warm, and the air so sweet with the smell of fresh-mown grass; or because the frogs and crickets are vying with each other as to which one can make the most racket, the young animals in pasture, the sky so high and clear with the stars and moon so far away one doesn't like to think that in a nuclear war they may be our only avenue of escape. No, this May is sweet to me because I have at last got rid of the letter. I no longer have to sit up night after night trying to compose it, then spend days wondering if I should mail it or not. What a waste of time that was. I knew from the beginning that I would mail it, I just had to work up the courage to do so. Because nobody has to tell me it's a fiendish thing, what I did. I know very well what's right and what's wrong. But right can be wrong and wrong can be right, if you understand the subtlety of what I'm trying to say. And in this case I think I was justified in doing what I did, although I know it's wrong to set myself up as a judge. Don't think for a moment that my conscience didn't bother me, but now that's all over. I feel liberated! Even happy. Sure, there were hours of remorse but they passed quickly, and the fact that Kent is worried fills me with satisfaction. I know he's worried, otherwise he wouldn't have hired Bill Ward.

I wonder — if he does — what way he will choose to commit suicide. Blow his brains out? Or run his car into a tree or a stone wall to make it look like an accident? By the way, I bought that blue paper at Bloomingdale's.

60

Thousands of people buy their stationery there and the salesgirls never look at a customer. They're always staring at their nails to see if the polish is chipped or if the new shade they've used is more becoming than the last one. I hate polished nails, never mind what color. Or they talk to each other and pay no attention to the customer, waiting patiently at the counter. They break it off when it suits them and not a minute before. Only in the food department is it different, but then there you get a number that assures you service when it's your turn.

It's odd to be writing a diary again. Writing a diary was the only consolation I had as a child. I found one in a garbage pail, an old-fashioned one, but it had never been written in. It reminded me of one my mother used to write in. Wonder what happened to that one? Guess it got chucked after my father died and I had to move on. Guess this one got chucked because the owner wanted a more modern one. "My Diary," in gold lettering, with a wreath of flowers around it. Corny. But good enough for me. The way we Americans throw things away . . . could help a lot of poor people. It may be less so now, but a few years ago you could almost furnish your house with the stuff in trashcans. Just because a screw was missing on a toaster or a radio, out it went. Half loaves of dry bread, fruit that maybe had a bad spot or two, which could have been cut out easily. And the furniture, put out on the street. Chairs, sofas that only needed a bit of new upholstery, or tables that needed a little refinishing here and there. Young couples used to scour the streets and pick up what they could use. I did it myself. Auctioneers do it. Then sell the stuff without fixing it, or fix up like new and make a bundle. But today . . . the kids go to those big furniture warehouses and buy stuff that doesn't hold up anywhere near as well as the old pieces. It just goes to show what kind of people we are. Too lazy to repair things ourselves because it's easier to buy something new, however crappy it is. People just don't know how to take care of things any more, or it doesn't seem worth while.

I think I forgot to mention . . . and I don't know why this comes to me now . . . that shortly after we moved again . . . and I got so sick of all this moving around . . . I helped steal a car. I didn't know it was being stolen; I thought the gang I got in with, and particularly Horace, just wanted to borrow it to give his girl a ride. Anyway, I was caught and booked as an accomplice. I was sent to Danbury. So was Horace. He told the judge that it had been my idea, and that was a lie. When we met in Danbury, I damn near killed him, but he had pals, and they ganged up on me. One night some of them got me and hung me head down over the toilet, with my head in the bowl and left me that way till the warden found me. I damn near died. After that there was nothing I wouldn't have done to make them suffer the way they'd made me suffer. All of us were cruel, and that's a fact. It was the only way to meet life in that kind of an institution, and there were always reasons to justify whatever you did. For instance, there was a dentist who used to drill our teeth quite unnecessarily, without any injection that might have made it less painful. In the end one of the boys killed him. It wasn't me.

Cruelty is something you can justify, and then again, you can't. It all depends on circumstances, or rather, I guess, on motive. What's driving you to be cruel. Sometimes, though, there are no motives, only opportunities. You come across a human being who's helpless and you realize your power, and something makes you want to exercise it, to see how strong you really are. Sometimes it's the very meekness of your victim, the fact that he doesn't put up a fight but seems to recognize in you something you didn't even know you had in you. A provocation. Sometimes the innate helplessness of a woman, a man, an animal, simply triggers it; sometimes an instinct, an urge actually, that what you have suffered others should suffer, makes you do things that are as loathsome as they are understandable. Anyway, I spent three years there and what I learned wasn't pretty. I don't know what impact it had on me, but I've often thought how easy it would be for me today to kill those sheep.

Thomas J. Kent. If he's going to kill himself, I think he'll do it while he's still on crutches. Once the cast is off his leg and he can move about freely again, he won't be a man who takes his life just because a crank wrote him a letter. I wish I knew how long his foot still has to be in a cast and if he'll be able to use his leg normally, once it's removed. Or will he still have to be careful? But I know that once he's back to normal again, his mind will no longer dwell on the accident of which he's reminded now, constantly, by his injuries. Once he starts flying again, he'll be as free as a bird.

I'll give him a few more weeks. Though they say it's easier to die in fall or winter than during spring or summer, when everything's so full of hope. But I can't wait until the autumn. I simply can't.

What a moon tonight, just like the night it shone on the dead sheep. But now it's almost June. The moonlight seems to come from far off, soft somehow. It shines on the white blossoms of the dogwood, and their dense leaves cast a solid shadow on the ground. They're blooming longer this year. Trees, like all plants, need nitrogen, phosphorus and potassium. Nitrogen makes for rapid growth of trunks and branches, and for healthy leaves; phosphorus helps the roots to grow; potassium strengthens them so that they can better withstand wind and ice, and are more resistant to disease. I learned that from my father. But then in this community almost everybody is tree-minded, has been long before 1924 when King's Point was finally incorporated as a village. All through those years people were concerned about keeping the environment as pleasant as possible. The trees and flowering shrubs John A. King brought back from his European travels are now recognized by the Long Island Horticultural Society as one of the most outstanding privately maintained collections still in existence. At least that's what the books say. But to get back to my father. If he had not died, things might have been different. All this being shunted around only to end up in jail. Or was it the end? I'm still around and the end, hopefully, is far away. For me. Not for Thomas J. Kent though. A few more weeks. Then I must act. But right now all I can do is wait, and that's something I've always found hard.

I I

Maximilian Forster rang for his valet to lock the apartment after him. It was a beautiful apartment, and he'd had some difficulty in buying it. The management didn't care to have foreigners living in their building, Jews were out of the question, and artists rarely given the privilege of occupying one of the few duplexes in the comparatively small building not far from the Metropolitan Museum of Art.

Forster had been born in Vienna and had managed to get away before Hitler had taken over. Not that he had had to escape the Nazis. He was not a Jew. His father had owned an art gallery, and upon his death in the late thirties, Maximilian had emigrated to New York with whatever art he had been able to salvage from his father's business, but had found the going difficult in that city and had moved to South America; from there to Mexico, where he had finally been successful in various ways, not always necessarily concerned with art. With considerably more means at his disposal, he had returned to the States and opened a small gallery on Madison Avenue which by now had several branches, in San Francisco and Miami, one in Paris and one in Geneva.

Maximilian's mother had been born into a well-to-do Turkish family, with one grandfather on her paternal side a Spaniard of some status in Spanish society. He had found out only later in life, when he was thirty odd years old, to what use these connections could be put. But then he really didn't like to recall the man who had stopped at his small shop in Mexico City one day and proposed to him that if he could procure a certain painting, an old master now owned by an impoverished family in Spain, and perhaps a few other items — no matter how, it should only be reasonable — then he wouldn't have to worry about money any more. Since that time, Forster had preferred to regard the connections he had made with relatives he had never cared about, sometimes not even sure how they spelled their names, as his own brainstorm.

While he waited in the small foyer for the elevator to come up, he looked at himself in the mirrored walls he had had put in to make the hall appear larger. He was not what one would have called a handsome man. Too short, too heavy, but his well-cut suits and the immaculate way he dressed lent him an air of quiet elegance. Waiters, women and policemen invariably recognized him at once as a very rich man. His face was bland, with no prominent features except his mouth, which was very full, his lips always as red as if he had used rouge on them. But what he hated about himself was his kinky hair which, from trying to flatten it, looked either too oily or too wet.

Maximilian strode quickly down Fifth Avenue, then turned sharply at the corner of Seventy-seventh Street and walked past his own gallery on Madison Avenue, which didn't look much from the outside, just one small showcase with two or three extraordinary gold statues in it behind an iron grille. On Mondays and Tuesdays it was closed, which suited everybody because it gave him and his employees a three-day weekend. In fall and winter, when the people who counted were back in the city, it was open until six on Fridays and Saturdays, otherwise until five. Of course, Maximilian could always be reached for personal appointments under his unlisted number, which only his important clients knew. And some of his closest friends. And Kitty. Not that he and Kitty were close, and at this moment Maximilian couldn't exactly recall why he had ever given it to her, except that he'd had a feeling that, headstrong as she was, she might run into trouble some day and need his help. Throughout the years they had stayed in contact, and once in a while, when she was in town, had met for luncheon or dinner. "Because," he told himself, "I got her picture on the front page of a magazine and she happened to be one of the few persons in my life who was grateful." But not until this morning had she ever phoned him and said, "I must see you urgently. Could you possibly make it around lunchtime?" He smiled. He was looking forward to meeting her again. Somehow he had never been able to altogether dismiss her from his mind. Childish perhaps to still feel frustrated about what had happened between them.

He entered the bar of the Carlisle, and there she was, sitting in a corner. "Your call," he said, "was a pleasant surprise. It must be a year, at least, since we last met."

Kitty looked up. "Is it really that long?"

The sight of him took her back to her days as an airline hostess. Many of her passengers had asked her for dates, but she had turned all of them down. Except Max. He had seemed to be a man who was not just playing around with pretty girls, but interested in her as a person. "You're much too lovely to be an airplane hostess," he'd said on that flight from Constantinople to Rome. "Why don't you try modeling? Even if it's only bras." He had told her what school to go to, found her a good, honest agent.

She had never quite been able to figure him out. He had connections everywhere. He was obviously well off — the way he lived, spent money, and in a way he was kind, always trying to help people, not only her, to achieve their goals. An elegant, well-bred man, erudite too. And always involved with women. The latter had killed a deeper relationship between them. He had almost thrown her out the night she had refused to sleep with him, but next morning had sent her a spray of white orchids, a card tucked in between. "As far as I'm concerned, I'll always be your friend."

It had touched her. She knew he was proud of his virility and not used to being turned down. She smiled at him, happy suddenly that she had called him. She had stood in line at the Met to get tickets for a performance, a birthday present for Kate. With the tickets finally in her hand, she had suddenly felt unreasonably depressed. By the time Kate's birthday came around, there might not be any cause for celebration. On an impulse she had walked to the nearest telephone booth and dialed Max.

66

Maximilian sat down and beckoned to the waiter. "Still like champagne?"

"Still adore it."

He ordered, and then said what she had expected him to say, "You look more beautiful than ever."

As a matter of fact, he thought, sizing her up from head to foot, it was true. At thirty-five — or was she already thirty-six? — she had come into full bloom. When he had seen her first, on the flight from Constantinople, she hadn't been very different from other pretty airline stewardesses, except there had been something about her that had spelled out quite clearly that she was different. He soon found out she had mind of her own and a set of values that wouldn't bend easily in the wind. He had never forgiven her for turning him down. Not because she had childishly slapped his face, he had been slapped before; not because she had given him a good kick in the groin which had hurt for days afterwards, but because, in spite of every kind of persuasion, she had adamantly refused to have sex with him. "If I want to make love to someone," she had told him, "I choose that person myself." And she had chosen Kent.

"You really do look more beautiful than ever," Maximilian repeated.

"I don't really." She was still smiling. She didn't know that it was her most attractive feature. It semed to start just below her small, narrow ears, run down her cheeks, up her nose and into her eyes, making them shine. "I couldn't be more beautiful than ever, not after standing in line for hours to get seats for the Bolshoi."

She had finished her drink; he asked her if she wanted another. When she declined, he helped her up from her chair, nodded slightly to the bartender who nodded in response, knowing Forster never paid but preferred to be sent a bill in spite of the fact that he knew it was padded. They walked down the few steps, through a door into a small lobby and from there into the dining room.

"I like it here," said Kitty, looking up at the porcelain

pieces in their niches, glad to have him sitting beside her. It was a wonderful distraction.

"Of course I read about the crash. Was terribly sorry. How is your husband?"

"We hope the cast can come off in two weeks. He's started to drive a little, just around town. It's his left foot."

"Glad to hear it." He was studying the menu. She remembered that he always ate sparingly, to keep his weight down, but had loved feeding her, and suddenly she was ravenous. When they had ordered their lunch, he leaned back and asked, "And now tell me, what can I do for you?"

"You haven't changed." Kitty shook her head. "You're still saying, 'What can I do for you?' "

"And you used to find that rude."

"No, I didn't. Well, not exactly. But I guess it used to put me on the defensive. I mean, a person asking what could he do for you, as if there always had to be a reason for calling or seeing anybody. But then it also made me feel sort of sorry for you, that you should think that unless somebody needed you, they wouldn't take the trouble to look you up."

There had been very few people who had ever felt sorry for him. His grandmother, perhaps, when he had had to appear in court on a count of fraud. Let go on probation. The stigma had rankled at the time. But since then he had erased this incident, like so many others, from his mind.

He looked at her hands. They were freshly manicured, good hands, strong, efficient, their nails slightly curved. Those lovely hands had slapped him and he had told her what a child she still was, how naive she was to expect a man not to make a pass at her when she came to his apartment. Wasn't she aware of her sensuality? Why was she trying to hide it?

"But now I have to repeat my question," he said. "What can I do for you? Because today *you* phoned *me* and wanted to see me, that it was urgent. So there must be something on your mind."

"There is," said Kitty. "I called you because I suddenly

68

felt strongly that what I need is advice from somebody objective, a sophisticated person, an outsider, and of all the people I could think of, you seemed to be the one to ask."

"Go ahead," he said. "What is it?"

But Kitty waited until the waiter had brought them the food. Then, between the hors d'oeuvre and the entree — a minute steak for her, nothing for him but a glass of red wine — she told him about the letter.

"We've engaged a private detective. A man called Bill Ward. Kent doesn't think much of him. He was on the force, and there was some gossip about him. He was to be downgraded, so he left. Now he's a private investigator. But I felt we had to do something, and Ward's supposed to be tops. The F.B.I. wants us to have Kate put under surveillance. What do you think?"

Maximilian shook his head. During the last fifteen years he had frequently found it necessary to resort to bodyguards and had always hated the feeling that his every move was being watched, even if only in a protective capacity, and there were nights when he had confused his own men with those who were keeping him under a quite different surveillance. "I wouldn't," he said, more firmly than he had intended. "It'll only make her feel the danger is real, and terrify her." And then, forgetting his usual caution, "I know what I'm talking about, because getting art out of a country, when it's considered a national treasure, is not always without danger, and I've had to resort to protection. Maybe you read about a case some years ago when a yacht loaded with antiquities was blown up shortly after it left harbor."

"Yours?"

"It belonged to a friend of mine. I had a few dealings with him."

When she had read about the boat, carrying artifacts from Turkey, exploding, Kitty had given a fleeting thought to Max, wondering if he could be involved in anything like that. But she hadn't really believed seriously that his business, among other things, could be smuggling. How naive of me, she thought.

69

"Well," said Max, "I hope your man is a crack detective as you say, because it's almost impossible to trace an anonymous letter. Thousands are written every day. Most people simply throw them out, unless there's a tip in them that might give the police a clue."

"No dessert," Kitty told the waiter. "Just coffee."

"Two," said Max. "And make it fresh and strong."

He turned back to Kitty. As he had noticed years ago, there was a little red mark just between her eyebrows, running down to the root of her proud little nose, a sign that she was excited. It had excited him because it had reminded him of a tiny, perfectly bred foal with a mark on its promising forehead.

She was unusually pale and her lips were trembling. A woman in despair. A woman who possibly hadn't made love for weeks on end.

"That letter," said Kitty, "didn't set a time limit. In a way that makes it even more menacing because it doesn't allow for any respite from anxiety. What if something happens to Kate?"

"Kate means a lot to you."

"Of course."

"More than your husband?"

"Sometimes I'm not sure."

He looked at her sharply. She was tapping the rim of her glass. "I wish the coffee would come. I've got to get home. After a while I always get restless and have to get back just to make sure everything's all right, and I hate to drive by myself when I feel as tired and worn out as I do right now."

"I tell you what," said Maximilian. "Let's have coffee at my place. Maybe I can help you."

"But you just said you couldn't. You said I shouldn't engage a bodyguard for Kate; the detective would possibly never trace the anonymous letter . . ."

"That's right," said Maximilian. "But you haven't really given me enough time to concentrate on the problem. To me just about everything can be straightened out if one puts one's mind to it. Let me try. But there's a lot more I'll have to know." He rose. "Let's go."

12

Kitty Kent drove home slowly and very carefully, at times even below the speed limit, and impatient drivers blew their horns and passed her on both sides. The speed of their cars passing hers created such suction, it blotted out the music on the radio. She closed the windows. There was no need yet to keep them open nor the air conditioning on. The late afternoon was cool. About twenty miles out of New York she stopped at a diner and went to the rest room. The two johns were taken, which didn't bother her. She stared at herself in the mirror above the dirty wash basins. There were deep shadows under her eyes that no amount of powder would cover. To erase them she needed a base cream. But she used so little make-up, she had nothing with her. Kent had always liked her to look natural, even preferred her without lipstick. "Most of them are scented," he said, "and after you've wiped your face you have to throw the handkerchief into the laundry."

She cleaned her face with one of the wash'n dries she always carried with her, then washed her hands. As usual, there were no paper towels left and she dried her hands on her pantyhose. She bought some mints at the candy counter. There were booths, but she squeezed into an empty seat at the counter. She ordered iced coffee and sipped it slowly through a straw. They say power corrupts, she thought, and absolute power corrupts absolutely. But what about terror? Absolute terror could also corrupt, probably because its source was power.

When Maximilian had first tried to sleep with her, it hadn't been on moral grounds that she had refused him. Today she recognized that it had been her ego that had made her reject him. It had gone against her pride to pay for something, call it a career if you wanted to, with sex, and to be left forever after with the feeling that you couldn't have made it on your own. She hadn't wanted to have an affair until she'd met Kent, and since her marriage she had never touched, kissed or gone to bed with another man. Why? Most of their friends did. There was quite a crowd, not far from where they lived, who found husband swopping amusing. She and Kent had steered clear of them. "Kitty with the iron pants." She couldn't remember who'd said it. The simple answer was that she had never felt the need for another male. Kent was good in bed, a zestful lover, and as long as she was satisfied . . . and she had been . . . it would have been like stuffing herself with outside food when she had plenty at home. That he had had other girls before her had seemed perfectly natural to her, also that once in a while he might go to bed with another woman when he was away. One day she had asked him outright if he did, and he had laughed. "I won't tell you."

"Why not?"

"Because it's none of your business, and it has nothing to do with my relationship with you."

"So what about honesty?" she had wanted to know.

"Honesty in that sort of thing," he had told her, "I don't call honesty. It's just unburdening yourself so you won't feel guilty and can tell yourself, well, she knows, so I gave her the chance to accept it or walk down the road."

"Maybe I want to be given that choice," she had said, but he had pretended not to hear. For him the subject had been closed.

How would he feel about an infidelity on her part? She knew that in a way he was old-fashioned enough to believe in a double standard for men and women where sex was concerned, although he might not want to admit it, that what a man could do without getting deeply attached, a woman couldn't. According to him, a woman's whole existence became involved when she gave herself to a man. Well, he was wrong.

She ordered another coffee, this time hot. It might clear her mind of all these surprising discoveries about herself.

72

She had gone reluctantly to Maximilian's apartment, with the apprehension that she was going to let happen what had happened. At first she had been furious that he was taking advantage of her despair. Cheap, she had thought, and had lain on the wide bed like a tree trunk, motionless, a silly joke coming to her mind about a bride on her wedding night with a note on her breast: "Go ahead. I'm chloroformed." But Maximilian, it had turned out, was an experienced lover with knowing hands, a combination of gentleness and brutality that had been able to make the tree trunk move. And it was this recognition that had thrown Kitty completely, the unexpected realization that it could be fun and satisfying with a man she didn't love.

"I had to be almost forty to find that out," she said aloud, shaking her head violently.

"Do you want anything else?" asked the waitress.

Kitty thanked her politely, left a much too large tip and walked out to the parking lot.

13

BILL WARD MUST have waited for Kent outside the hospital. Anyway, he was there when Kent left it. "Aha," he said. "A walking cast."

"Yes," said Kent. "But I have to use the crutches a week longer and not put my full weight on my left foot yet. But I may drive."

"You've been driving already."

Kent grinned. "I know. But without permission. God, how my muscles have atrophied. And in such a short time. Unbelievable." He was scanning the parking lot for Kitty's car. Usually she was on time.

"Bill," he said. "The other day you seemed to think it almost impossible to find the writer of an anonymous letter."

"Well, it depends on luck. With some dames you come, with some you don't. Luck's what you need. Who said it? I think it was Edison. In the first place, luck. In the second place, luck. In the third place, more luck. And when it comes to luck, my record's good. You should be paying me more. Now . . . let's start with the survivors . . . Get in. Sit down. Want me to drive you home?"

Kent got in beside Bill Ward, let down the window on his side. "No, that's all right, thanks. Kitty should be here any minute. You were saying, the survivors . . ."

"The most likely one we have is Anna Barlov."

"She's out," said Kent.

"Granted. But what about her father?"

Kent frowned. It had occurred to him, then he had dismissed the thought.

"And then there's Gilbert Gordon, who was also hurt. Quite critically for a while, but they say he'll make a full recovery. Okay. But he's a pal of Anna Barlov's."

"Pal?"

74

Bill Ward's laugh was more a snort. "Do you think she could live in the style she's living in on what *she* makes? And that father of hers looks as if he's always been a poor fish."

For some strange reason, Kent was surprised. He couldn't quite believe that Gilbert Gordon's relationship with Anna was that intimate, but it could be true. He was probably being naive.

"And then there's the old dame in New York, Helga Johnson."

"Somehow I can't see a woman writing that letter Sam agreed with me."

"Women can be more fiendish than men, but I'd leave her on the list. And then there's the guy in Newark, New Jersey. Cramer. Never knew anything good to come out of Newark. But from what I've found out about him, he doesn't seem likely. He's suing for a million bucks and seems to be enjoying it. Never in his life could have hoped for anything near that amount of dough. For him the crash was a windfall."

Kent shuddered at the thought that anyone could happily seek compensation from such a disaster, but it figured, in today's world.

"But there's one question I wanted to ask you," said Bill Ward. "What was your relationship with your co-pilot, Henderson?"

Kent shook his head. "Not relationship. He's older than I am. Sometimes I had the feeling that he resented my being a captain. He was known as a weak pilot. Maybe I was a bit too stern with him, and quite often impatient. But I don't think him capable of writing such a letter, not of doing such a crazy thing."

"He knows your home address, and that you have a daughter called Kate?"

"Yes. He's been at the house once or twice. His visits weren't exactly a success."

"In what way?"

Kent shrugged. "He's just not a very sociable person, I guess. Came late, left early, leaving no impression on anyone present. The last time he spent at our house was

75

the night of the crash. He got away with just a few minor cuts and bruises."

"I wouldn't rule him out."

"I don't," said Kent. "On the contrary — he was one of the first people to come to my mind."

"I suggest you have a talk with him."

"I wanted to." Kent sighed. "I called his home and spoke to his wife, who sounded agitated. He hasn't gone back to flying. He's in the hospital."

"I thought you said he wasn't hurt."

"It seems he's had a nervous breakdown. And some sort of accident. He's in Hartford General. I got hold of his psychiatrist but he was adamant about my not seeing Henderson until he was released. He said he'd call me as soon as he is."

"And then," Bill Ward went on, "in Philadelphia there's Harry Summerfield. He and his three sons survived, but he lost his wife and only daughter in the crash. Only daughter ... see the connection?"

Kent's mind wasn't gaited that way, but he saw the connection.

"Summerfield's a Jew. Refugee. In my opinion Jews always carry a chip on their shoulders. According to the F.B.I. Summerfield's son was trying to find out your address. I think they'll be the first ones I'll take on."

There was a silence. Then Kent said, "Ward, would you mind if I took on these people you just mentioned? I'm not doubting your ability in any way; I just feel they might have the same reaction I'd have if an utter stranger came to my house to question me. Whereas I, the pilot of the plane ... I mean, it would be almost a natural thing for me to call on them to express my sympathy. I'd be able to form some sort of opinion, after which you could take over."

"I can't say I like the idea," said Ward, "because ..." he hesitated, shook his head, sighed and shrugged. "Anyhow, it'll give you something to do instead of sitting on your ass and waiting for us to come up with something. Go ahead. Report to me right away. And you have my blessing. Here comes your wife."

76

14

THEY WERE HAVING breakfast. Kate had left for school. Kitty reached for Kent's cigarettes. He handed her the package. He hated to see that she had acquired the miserable habit.

She lighted the cigarette, inhaled deeply; he waited, it seemed ages for a faint puff of smoke to leave her lips. "Things aren't right between us," she said. "Ever since that letter came, there's a new element, a sort of franticness in our lovemaking. As if we were using each other to distract ourselves from what worries us. At least that's my feeling."

It was true, thought Kent. In bed they'd become simply male and female, seeking relief instead of the sweetness of intimacy. And in their daily talk neither of them could avoid mentioning the danger that threatened Kate, unless ... The word unless had taken on a dreadful meaning.

"I know we can't let this thing drive us crazy," he said slowly, "but I just can't sit around and wait."

"So what more can we do?"

"I want Kate put under surveillance."

"Not yet. Please, Kent, not yet. It would unnerve her. I know it would. So far she doesn't seem to be giving the thing a thought."

He got up. "I'm going over to see Anna. Her father upset me."

'You don't think he ..."

'I don't think anything. I just have to do something."

"I'll drive you over."

"No. I'll drive myself."

Anna lived in a small, one-storey house about a mile down the road from theirs. She had leased it with the condition that the rent would count toward the eventual price of the property, should she want to buy it. Kent thought of what Ward had said. With rentals what they were today, it did seem unlikely . . .

The house had a large living room, divided by a tall screen behind which was an empty space, a practice bar, one wall mirrored . . . She had done nothing as yet to change it. There were two bedrooms, a bath between, a large kitchen with dining area, but it was the grounds that were so attractive, not quite two acres, surrounded by a high hedge that kept it hidden from view. Half of the garden was planted with flowering shrubs and unusual plants, and a narrow, gravel path ran through it. The other section was carpeted with wild flowers.

Anna was lying in the sun on a deck chair, her amputated leg covered with a plaid. Next to it lay a contraption of steel, with some leather straps. "It's still painful," she said. "The therapist showed me how to strap it on and helped me to walk around, but after ten minutes I had to give up. Tomorrow I'll exercise for twenty minutes, come hell or high water. She told me it's worse to lose an arm, that it throws you off balance. But my dancing helps. After all, I've had to do plenty on one leg in adagio. But you know, I can really do better without it. No, that's not true, but on the crutches I felt so secure. With this thing . . . I have a feeling it might come off and I'll fall flat on my face. Where it goes around my knee, it's like an iron ribbon, like something from the Middle Ages. Oh well, I'll get used to it."

She broke off abruptly, as if ashamed to have complained at such length to Kent. She smiled at him. "Thank God you didn't have any complications."

Kent knew he had been lucky, but faced with Anna's incapacitation, it was no consolation. "I was spared a lot of suffering," he told her, "but I don't have to tell you how I feel about what you've had to go through."

"It wasn't your fault," said Anna. "Oh, Thomas, how often do I have to assure you that I don't hold you responsible in any way. I didn't need any investigation to tell me that."

"Apparently there are people who don't agree with you."

"Idiots!"

"Possibly. But in a way I can understand their feeling of frustration, even a certain urge to avenge themselves on a fate I couldn't prevent."

"I can't imagine anybody wanting to get back at you for something you couldn't possibly help."

"May I be completely honest with you?"

"But you always have been," said Anna. "Even when I told you I was in love with you and would like to sleep with you."

"Did you really say that?"

"I said that, and you remember it very well, and I remember very well what you answered. You said, 'You are more beautiful than Kitty, but marriage is a contract, and I don't break contracts easily. I may sometimes dream of holding you in my arms, but in the end I would only hurt you because I couldn't consider it anything but a passing affair.'"

"Was I as brutal as that?"

"You were honest," said Anna. "You wanted me. There was never any doubt in my mind about that. Don't tell me you've also forgotten the night you came by on your way from the airport. You phoned me to say you were coming. I opened the door to you almost nude, and you said you were sorry you'd come too early, and left."

"No, I've not forgotten that," he said.

"You resented my crudeness, my aggressiveness. I still remember your face. But that's the way I'm made. I've always gone after what I wanted. If it weren't for my leg, I'd sit on your doorstep day in and day out, trying . . . no, I wouldn't. Because Kitty was my first friend out here, the only person who would give me a nod, and she's never stopped being friendly, even though she must know by now that we wanted each other. And there's something about that kind of generosity that can only be repaid by generosity. So I've been trying to dismiss you from my mind. It's difficult, I admit. In you I would have found a man who'd let me live the way I wanted to, who wouldn't have resented my ambition but understood it, even been proud of it, and I could have let you see as much as you wanted of other women — passengers, hostesses, girls in foreign cities, and I wouldn't have given a damn, as long as you were coming home to me. As you come home to Kitty. I know better now. You're . . . don't be offended, but you're not what I would call sexy. I am. But you can take it or leave it, depending on your mood. If you'd ever slept with me, you wouldn't have needed any other woman. Yes, Thomas, I still love you, although you can be quite a bore, as most men with high moral standards are. To sleep with somebody a night or two, okay. Or am I overestimating you? But you don't go in for affairs. You are, my dear, quite old-fashioned. But you've got integrity, and that, I think beside your good looks, is one of the things that attracted me most to you." She paused, closed her eyes. "Get me a lemonade or some iced tea. My throat is dry from this long explanation, which was quite uncalled for."

"I hope I don't run into your old man," said Kent, rising.

"You won't. He's gone to the city. Again. To see if he can make any headway with the lawyer. He was a man who never could wait, and now . . . It seems to be the only thing he has left to look forward to since my becoming a prima ballerina is out."

Kent went into the kitchen, squeezed some oranges and limes into a glass, put in some ice and brought it out to her. "I fixed myself a martini. I hope you don't mind."

"You're drinking too much, Thomas. Why not just have some white wine with soda water?"

"You're quite right," he nodded. "I've been drinking too much. It worries Kitty, and Kate's taking to hiding the liquor in her closet."

"There was something you were going to tell me, and I quite forgot to ask what. Pain makes you so terribly preoccupied with yourself. What was it?"

Kent pulled out the Xeroxed copy of the letter and handed it to her. Anna read it slowly. When she handed it back to him, her hand was shaking. "Pretty frightening."

"Yes. It frightened Kitty. I don't know what impression it made on Kate."

"Kate?"

"Yes. She found it and read it. We would have had to tell her anyway."

"How does she feel about it?"

"As far as Kitty and I can make out, she doesn't feel about it at all, and as far as she's concerned, we pretend it doesn't bother us."

"And why are you showing it to me, Thomas? You wouldn't want to frighten me if you didn't feel it was necessary. So . . . why?"

For a moment there was silence between them.

"Why?" Anna asked again.

"I took the letter to the F.B.I. They kept the original, that's why all I have is the Xeroxed copy. The original was on blue notepaper, and the block letters were in red. They seemed to think the tiles of a scrabble set had been used. And the letter was addressed to me, here . . . so . . . they feel it must be someone who knows me, someone who wants to even a score with me."

He paused. Anna sat up in her chair. "And you suspect my father," she said, her voice as calm as usual. But then, quite suddenly, she laughed, and just as suddenly stopped laughing. "He's never seen a scrabble set in his life. If he heard someone mention it, he'd think it was some Southern dish."

Kent said nothing.

Anna threw off the plaid that covered her stump. "Take a good look at it," she said, "and try to understand him. He looks at it every hour on the hour. Sometimes he moans, sometimes he cries, Sometimes he just runs out of the room. The only person who can calm him is Father Ambrosius. You know, faith — if you have it, is a wonderful help. I simply cannot imagine him writing a letter like this. I know there isn't a thing in the world he wouldn't do for me, and has done; so did my mother. They denied themselves every smallest luxury to pay for my lessons. Oh, I got scholarships, but then there were all the things I needed — ballet shoes, leotards, tights, besides just our daily living. And when I began to work, it didn't even begin to cover what I was using up. We lived on a farm with relatives and moved to the city because of me, where it was even harder to make a living. He washed dishes, collected garbage, always regretting that he hadn't learned a trade that would have enabled him to maintain some sort of dignity. My mother went out to cook, took in fancy ironing, then she died quite suddenly. From sheer exhaustion, said the doctors."

"But is he a vengeful man?"

Anna hesitated. "Vengeful? I think he believes in an eye for an eye and a tooth for a tooth, but to write a letter like that? Impossible. Of course he knows that I love you and can't have you on my own terms. If you were dead, I suppose he thinks I'd stop longing for you. But why would he threaten Kate?"

She fell silent. Kent said, "She's my only daughter, and she's blessedly whole."

Anna stared at him, wide-eyed. "And if you're to stay alive, he wants to see you suffer just as he is suffering, seeing me . . . Is that what you think? She sat up abruptly. "If that is so . . . then he's sick. I know what I'll do. I'll go see Father Ambrosius and talk to him about it."

"Let me go," said Kent.

She fell back, as if defeated. "Go," she said. "But I'm going to send him back to Louisville."

"But then you'll be all alone."

"I'll get a housekeeper. If worse comes to worst, I'll marry Gilbert Gordon."

"Gilbert Gordon?"

"He's played an important role in my life these past years. Do you think I could live like this, do you think I could have afforded nurses around the clock on what my father and mother did for me, or on what I was able to make?"

"Do you love him?"

"I'm very fond of him. But you're the only right man for me. But I can't have you. I bitterly regret it, but I don't regret having told you in plain words what you must have guessed anyway from my behavior."

It was then that Kent took her in his arms. After he had left, Anna cried for a long time.

15

FATHER AMBROSIUS' CHURCH was located in an old-fashioned building, erected in the early twentieth century, with the rectory adjacent to it. A very old lady opened the door, apparently the Father's housekeeper. She led Kent through a small hall — a bench on the left side, a coat stand on the right — on a shelf above it dangled half a dozen different colored wigs. Noticing that Kent was looking at them in surprise, she smiled. "Father Ambrosius uses them instead of a hat or cap, since he lost his hair a few years ago. And what a mane he had!"

The room he was asked to wait in was overloaded with incongruous, old pieces, Victorian, possibly the real thing. The backs and arms of chairs and sofa were protected with antimacassars. To Kent they looked like pieces of Kleenex. He sat down on a chair that seemed to be the most comfortable one to him. It was hard, stuffed undoubtedly with horsehair, and upholstered in black, shiny material. After a few minutes he was asked to enter the priest's study and was astonished by the contrast of ultra-modern, functional furniture, all chrome and leather, which gave the room a light and airy atmosphere, except for a small niche between the two windows that held a carved, painted madonna, a votive light flickering underneath. Father Ambrosius rose from behind his writing desk. He was an unexpectedly tall, good-looking man in his early sixties. The camel-hair robe he was wearing looked worn and faded from many cleanings.

"Excuse me for not being properly dressed," he said, "but the church was cold, as it always is early in the morning, and since I'm just recovering from a bout of flu I feel the cold, even at this time of the year. But you made it sound so urgent, Mr. Kent, I thought you wouldn't mind."

"I certainly do not, Father."

The priest pointed to the chair opposite the marble-covered desk. As Kent sat down, he asked, "And what brings you to me, my son?"

Kent took out his pipe, hesitated, but the priest pushed an ashtray across to him. 'Go ahead and smoke if it makes it easier for you to talk."

Kent stuffed his pipe, lighted it. He felt the Father's eyes resting on him with a warmth that gave him an unexpected feeling of peace.

"Stanislav Barlov," he said. "Anna Barlov's father. He hates me."

"I know," said Father Ambrosius. "And I believe his hatred is based primarily on the attitude you have taken toward the whole tragedy as simply one of the hazards of flying."

"Well, in a way it is."

"But he can't see it that way, nor can he accept the fact that you were made the instrument of death by God's will. And that therefore he has to accept it. I've had many talks with him."

"Anna told me yesterday that her father believes in revenge . . . an eye for an eye, a tooth for a tooth. I have a letter with me which I received earlier this week and I wonder if you would be good enough to read it."

He took the Xeroxed copy out of his pocket and pushed it across the desk. Father Ambrosius picked it up, unfolded it and read it, put it down, picked it up again, this time putting on his glasses. His thin lips moved silently as he read it for a second time, then he put it down slowly, shaking his head. "How very terrible."

"Indeed it is," said Kent. "At first I wanted to ignore it, but since my daughter is threatened, I felt I couldn't. I went to the F.B.I., that's why I don't have the original. One thing that bothers me is the demand that I 'redeem' myself. Anna's father used just that expression the other day. What I came to ask you is — do you think it is possible that he could have written the letter? I've been

84

told he went out of his mind, practically, when he saw what had happened to his daughter."

Father Ambrosius nodded. "I know. Poor man. But it is understandable. Try to imagine yourself in his situation, a beloved daughter disabled, her career ruined."

"I have," said Kent. "That's why I'm here. But I can't imagine myself, even in his circumstances, threatening a man with the demand that he commit suicide or his child will be harmed."

"Nor could Stanislav Barlov," said Father Ambrosius. "No matter how deeply he was shocked to see all his hopes for Anna shattered, no matter how much he blames you or perhaps, in moments of derangement, feels the need to revenge himself on you . . . he is not an evil man, not a man — and I think I know him well enough to judge him — who would do anything like this."

"Anna is going to send him back to Louisville."

"A good idea. He'll be spared the daily sight of his daughter. A good psychiatrist might help too." Suddenly his eyes bored into Kent. "Allow me one question, my son. Do you feel guilty?"

"Guilty? No. I did the best I could and more no man can do."

Actually he hadn't pondered the question before. Had he been arrogant to believe he could bring off the landing successfully, trusted too much to his experience, his faith in his skill and luck? "But if you say it was God's will that I crash my plane," he said, suddenly on the defensive, "then it was also God's will that twenty people would die and so many others be injured. But, Father, I am not a religious man."

Father Ambrosius smiled. "Don't you regard religion as a kind of philosophy, Mr. Kent?"

"Certainly. For me that's all there is to it. A crutch to lean on for people not strong enough to cope with their problems. Just as other people lean on other philosophies in order to be able to bear life. To be in harmony with yourself and the universe is what counts."

Father Ambrosius leaned back in his chair. "I wonder — are you truly in harmony with yourself since the crash?

Are you sure you did your best? To me it seems — if I may say so — almost impertinent. And now . . ." He pointed to the letter in front of him. "Haven't you come to me, perhaps, because you are in need of what so many people like you call a crutch, just because so many people grasp it? Do you honestly believe that philosophy is not a crutch, a thought process as valid as faith, that helps us to keep some sort of mental balance? If you think I believe in hell, a hell down below, you are mistaken. I think of hell as our time on earth and of heaven as a relief from the afflictions that are imposed on us while we are alive." He paused. "But ultimately a man has to stress his relationship with God, or if you want to call it the universe, or the Great Power that created us all. Therefore, I cannot understand why the word redeem should bother you so. You say you do not feel guilty, very well, but I certainly believe you should feel the deepest regret."

"But I do. I regret it deeply."

"I am glad to hear that. Because regret is a source for renewed life. It gives me great satisfaction to help solve the doubts of modern man. We have managed to conquer the moon, but not to heal cancer and other fatal sicknesses. We are ahead in thousands of technical ways, but human nature hasn't changed since the world was created. Hatred, greed, envy still exist. Sacrifice, even if you don't believe that the Savior made the supreme sacrifice for humanity, is still an example. In my opinion we have to learn to sacrifice ourselves for the good of all."

"Are you trying to tell me, Father, that I should make a sacrifice of myself, as the letter implies?"

Father Ambrosius shook his head, but his face was suddenly stern. "It is not for me nor for anyone else to tell a man how he may redeem himself. All I am trying to say is that I believe the powers that rule our stay on earth are trying to teach us something — what I cannot tell. I wish I could. I only know that nothing would make sense to me if I couldn't believe there was a reason behind it all, even if we can't recognize it." He interrupted himself. "Sorry. I know you didn't come to me to hear a sermon. As for your question, I can only say again, I think it is

86

impossible that Stanislav Barlov wrote this letter."

He picked it up from where it still lay on the highly polished marble-top of his desk, and read it for a third time, this time aloud. "To my mind," he said finally, "this letter has been written by a man with a sick mind, by someone who wants to take revenge for something he was forced to do, something that may have deflected him, or that he thinks deflected him from being a good man. A man who hates or envies those who possess what he has been striving for and has not been able to achieve, who will not accept the fact that his capabilities may be less than those of others. An insecure man, with a low opinion of himself. He could have picked on thousands of other people who had better chances, more money, status, all of which he may be missing. Why, I wonder, did he pick on you? Do you know anyone, a person who has been jealous of you for reasons real or imaginary, who might want to settle a personal account with you, however deranged?"

"I could think of quite a few people," said Kent, "who envy me or have envied me." Henderson, he thought. "I've had an exceptionally good life. My father was a distinguished pilot, a world war ace, so everyone took for granted that I would follow in his footsteps. There was always enough money. I was presentable; girls liked me. I can't remember ever having been turned down. I'm married to a lovely woman who loves me; I have a child we both adore, a good salary, and got away from the crash with minor injuries."

"I am often puzzled," said Father Ambrosius, "when I see with whom my parishioners choose to identify themselves, or whom they regard as a demon who should be eliminated. It has nothing to do with intelligence or stupidity. It's something deep in their make-up, a childhood experience perhaps, that left its mark. Sometimes even a prenatal experience. In former days a priest fulfilled the part psychiatry plays now; confession and the punishment meted out for immoral behavior relieved their guilt. I have known quite a few priests who, in my opinion, did as well, better, than some psychiatrists I have heard about. I have always regretted that my theological

87

training did not include psychology. Today, of course, it does."

Father Ambrosius rose. "I can only repeat what I said before : there are many people whose basest instincts can be triggered by some incomprehensible incident. Given the opportunity they will beat a man to death or gas him or kill him by mental torture." He held out his hand. "Whenever you feel like a talk, come and see me. Even if it leads nowhere. I'm sorry I failed you."

'But you didn't, Father. You have assured me that Anna Barlov's father couldn't possibly be a suspect."

16

"There was a call for you from Hartford," Kitty told him, when Kent came back from Father Ambrosius. "I left the operator's number on your desk."

It took only a few minutes to get through to Henderson's psychiatrist. "I promised to call you when I thought my patient was fit enough to see you. He's home. You can visit him at your convenience. Try not to upset him."

Kent breathed a sigh of relief. There were no urgent appointments to keep him from leaving right away. "I'm going to drive up to Winsted to see Henderson," he told Kitty.

"It's a long drive. Three hours at least. Let me drive you."

"No," he said, "You stay here with Kate. I may have to stay the night." It was a brilliant day, even the Sound was sparkling, the green was still fresh, and as he drew closer to the Litchfield Hills, the scenery became more enchanting. The dreariness of industrial Winsted however was a sharp contrast. He passed through it and out into the rural area where Charlie Henderson lived, on a small farm that wasn't worked any longer. The petals of the dogwood, pink and white, were browning on the ground, the berries already forming; the laurel was in full bloom and the wisteria, climbing up the house, was a lavender cascade. But there was nothing enviable about the one-storey house. The front door opened into a large, drab living room. To the right was a modern kitchen with a service window toward the dining area; to the left a narrow passage with two doors. One of them opened quietly when Kent walked in, after ringing three times. The door wasn't locked. A nurse in white uniform appeared, a psychiatric nurse, according to the doctor.

"It's Mr. Kent, isn't it? Dr. Willowby advised us that you'd come at eleven." She glanced at her watch. "You're on time." Her voice was gentle but authoritative The next moment another voice yelled loudly through the second door in the corridor. "Tell him to go away. I don't want Charlie to see him."

A woman in a short, flowered nightgown appeared, her hair disarranged, her hands fluttering like a frightened bird. She was trying to hide her face. Then suddenly, her hands were quiet, fell to her side. The voice though, remained the same, high-pitched, hysterical. "I hate you," she screamed. "I hate you for what you did to Charlie and me. You made him lose his mind. Weeks in an institution when they wouldn't let me see him."

"I'm very sorry," said Kent. "But there's no telling how people will react to an accident as serious as this one. Some do lose their minds for a while. All I can say is, I'm sorry."

"Why don't you go back to bed, Mrs. Henderson," said the nurse. "I'll bring you your cocoa in a moment."

"I want you to spare Charlie having to see this monster." She turned to Kent again. "He jumped out of the window and fractured both legs. It was your fault. He broke his arm; it was your fault. What kind of a life can he lead, crippled? What kind of a life am I going to lead?"

"Mr. Kent didn't make your husband injure himself," the nurse said gently. "It was a miracle the fall didn't kill him. It was the fault of the attendants, not Mr. Kent's. And he won't always be a cripple."

Mrs. Henderson wouldn't let her go on. "You idiot! It's still his fault. It's all the consequence of his crashing the plane. Charlie was out of his mind when he jumped, and why did he lose his reason? Because Mr. Kent crashed their plane. Go away," she turned to Kent. "Get out of my house."

The nurse took Mrs. Henderson's arm and led her gently back to her room, calling over her shoulder, "I'll be back in a sec."

She was. "I've given her a hypo. But I'm afraid you

won't find my patient in much better condition. Of course she's no help. He should go to a nursing home and not have to cope with her hysteria, rubbing it in day after day that he's . . . useless."

She nodded in the direction of a door Kent had overlooked. It led from the living room into a small studio, not unlike his "cage". Here, too, the walls were hung with maps and flight schedules, and a big antique globe stood next to the armchair in which Henderson was sitting. Both his legs were in casts. He looked even smaller than he was, a thin wiry man. His face showed the same tension, the same anxiety it always had. Kent had never understood why Henderson had chosen to be a pilot when he was even afraid of riding a bicycle in traffic. Yet Henderson had volunteered for Vietnam in '64. Why? To prove himself? To overcome his fear? Or because he wanted to feel almighty, bombing and strafing defenceless people, hating them because they were as defenceless as he was?

"So there you are," he said. "Come to gloat over what you've done to me."

His voice hadn't changed. It was the voice of a boy in puberty. Suddenly Kent remembered that Henderson had always sung well. He said, "Nothing could be further from my mind."

How often — even before the crash — had he blamed Henderson for his professional inability. He had made countless mistakes in radio transmission, had had to be given repeated instructions by the aircraft controller, and he had certainly been a confused witness at the investigation probing the crew's training experience. There was no point now though in rubbing it in. Charlie Henderson had reacted to the whole thing with a nervous breakdown. Kent's trauma of the broken hip had lasted only a short while. But he had had Kitty and Kate, while all Charlie had was a hysterical wife.

"You never liked me," Henderson said bitterly. "I know you tried to get someone else for your co-pilot."

Kent refrained with some difficulty from answering back, "It was you who didn't like me, because you're older, and because you failed twice to get upgraded to captain."

"Why do you blame me?" Kent asked. "You know I did the best I could."

"But you didn't," said Henderson. "It was your decision to land at Kennedy, but you had the choice of turning around and landing in Washington instead. Or don't you remember? Have you conveniently forgotten? Your alternate was Washington, where the weather was less severe, but you decided for Kennedy."

"At the time," Kent said quietly, "my decision not to go to Washington was based on the fact that at that particular time, wheather had not reached minimums. And you know that as well as I do. The indication implied improvement in the weather at Kennedy. And, as you well know, we also had the fuel situation. And in Kennedy we had a better chance to have the gear problem checked."

"You didn't divert the plane to Washington while you still had the chance. And nothing of this alternative was ever mentioned. You weren't even criticized for it by the NTSB. You even got a citation for your skillful landing. And that's a laugh. I'd like to know how much it cost you."

Kent couldn't contain his rage. "You know damn well, Charlie, that I made a perfect landing. We touched down at exactly the right spot, at the exact speed . . ."

"But whose decision was it to try Kennedy instead of diverting the flight to Washington?"

It was only then, standing opposite Charlie Henderson, who would never have dared to say yes or no to anything that might commit him or put some kind of responsibility on him, that it struck Kent why he had taken the letter seriously. He knew what had harassed him through all the weeks of his own injuries, and since the letter — the fact that no other people but the airline, the Board and Charlie could know that he had been given a choice to divert the flight, that the letter might very well have been written by somebody who, like Charlie, blamed him for having made the wrong decision and therefore caused the crash. His injury dated from after the letter had been sent. It *was* possible. He would have to pass on his suspicion to the F.B.I. and to Bill Ward. He closed his eyes for a moment as something akin to a feeling of sickness overwhelmed him. This having to point a finger, without really knowing . . . but what other recourse did he have? Nobody was going to come forward and say, "I wrote the letter." The only way was to follow up a suspicion, however faint.

"Is there anything I could possibly do for you?" he asked.

"You phrased that okay," said Charlie Henderson. "There isn't anything you could possibly do for me. You've done your bit on me."

17

"THANK GOD YOU'RE back," said Kitty. "I've never been afraid before, but I was restless all night and got hardly any sleep. All of a sudden I heard noises I've never heard before. I know it's nonsense, but I can't help it. So what did you find out about Henderson?"

"I think it's possible that he might have written the letter. He accused me of all sorts of things which weren't true. Or perhaps his wife, who seems just as mentally disturbed. For the first time it occurred to me that a woman might be behind the whole thing. Ward wouldn't rule it out. I called the F.B.I. from Winsted. Now I've got to talk to Ward."

After making the call to Ward, he told Kitty, 'Tomorrow I'm going to Philadelphia to see Harry Summerfield. It's Sunday. That might be a good day to find him in, but if I don't, I'll stay the night."

"Take us with you," Kitty begged. "I really don't want to be alone with Kate again overnight."

Kent thought for a moment, then picked up the phone. "Who are you calling? Not the police, I hope."

"No. Sam. I'm sure he won't mind sleeping here and spending whatever time he has during the day at our place."

"Funny," said Kitty. "I never thought of him."

Summerfield's apartment was in one of those terrible buildings that looked from the outside like a barracks or an old-fashioned prison. And not much better inside. Uniformed guards with dogs on the leash walked along the narrow corridors, and although Kent had pressed the buzzer outside the front door and had waited for the voice asking who he was and why he wanted to see Mr. Summerfield, he was again asked where he was going. On the eighth floor he was met at the elevator by a boy of about fourteen. He introduced himself as Eugene Summerfield. "Mr. Kent?" he asked, and when Kent nodded, the boy pointed to a door on his right. "Apartment 81 C," and walked a few steps ahead of Kent. He opened the door to a tiny hall that led into the living room which held two worn couches, a writing desk near the window, some bookshelves and stacks of paper and books all over the floor. A dog growled and was silenced by a sharp command from behind a folding door that evidently led to the kitchen. "Just a minute," another boy's voice rang out. "I'm almost through feeding Father."

A seeing-eye dog came forward and sniffed at Kent. "Lie down, Milo," said the boy who had introduced himself as Eugene, and to Kent, "Please sit down." He helped Kent politely into one of the two chairs, and disappeared.

A minute later Harry Summerfield came in, leaning heavily on the arm of the boy who had called out to Kent to wait. He was of small build, with a high forehead and a nose that sprang into his face, strong and crooked at the root. The dark green glasses he was wearing covered almost half of his narrow face. His age was hard to guess. He seemed a lot older than Kent had been led to believe.

"I hear you are the pilot who was unfortunate enough to crash our plane. I am glad you survived. Gene told me you were still on crutches. I hope you will soon be able to walk without them. Walter, is this my chair?" His voice was soft and gentle, although colored by a strong German accent.

Walter, about two years older than Eugene, nodded, remembered that his father couldn't see the gesture and said, "Yes, Dad, that's your chair."

Mr. Summerfield sat down carefully, first touching the rim of the chair to make sure it was there, then he stretched his legs far out, but pulled them back when they hit a stack of papers, and asked, "Why do you want to see me?"

Kent forgot about the letter in his pocket. Impossible that this man could have written or dictated it to any of his sons.

"I happened to be in Philadelphia," said Kent, "and

since you were one of my unfortunate passengers, I thought I would come up to tell you how sorry I am that..."

"But it was not your fault," said Harry Summerfield. "And it is very good of you to take the trouble to see me. You are quite young, aren't you, Mr. Kent? At least your voice sounds young to me. I hope the crash will not leave you with a trauma, so that you can go back to flying as soon as you are able to."

The two boys had sat down on the floor. "Perhaps Mr. Kent can tell us when the compensation will come in," said Walter, and turning to Kent, "the lawyer we have seems to be terribly slow. Perhaps you could put a word in with the line..."

Kent didn't know what to say. Though the investigation of the NTSB had started almost immediately after the crash, the settling of compensations could go on for years, and there was no way of telling how long it might take for the people who had no personal insurance to receive their claims. Any airline was of course insured against the passenger suing, but... avoiding a direct answer therefore he said, "You didn't by chance buy any insurance?"

"I didn't," said Summerfield. "It was stupid of me, but frankly, I didn't even think of it. If I had been flying alone, or if all of us hadn't been on the plane, it might have occurred to me. But with the whole family on board .... that we didn't all die... for me, what would it have mattered, but for the boys? Yes, if only I had taken out insurance, it would be easier for us today, at least financially."

"We were all so excited," interrupted Eugene. "You see, it was our first flight. Mama had contracted some relatives through a German paper. We wanted to meet them, we were going down some day by bus, but then their oldest son got married and they wanted us at the wedding and they sent us the plane tickets, round trip. And then..." his voice faltered.

"I suppose you know," said Walter, "that our mother and sister didn't survive."

Kent knew. He had taken the trouble to find out every-

96

thing he could about this family before coming to see them. "I couldn't be more sorry," he said, and wondered which one of the boys had wanted to find out where he lived. Certainly not these two. Whoever was in the kitchen...

"And now Walter is the *Hausfrau*," said Gene, "and he's better at it than any of us expected. He's a good cook. And I take Dad to the disability claim office."

"Otherwise," said Walter, "all he can do is sit around and grieve."

"Jews have been forced to grieve through centuries." Summerfield smiled in a way that touched Kent almost unbearably.

"I understood you had a good job as copy editor at the *Enquirer*."

"That's gone, of course," said Summerfield. "Although the people, I mean my employers, have been very good to me. My severance pay is keeping us going, for the present. That, and the disability payments. But I've got to think ...what can a blind man do? You see, the fire ruined the optic nerve in both eyes. But let's not talk about that. I have my three boys left and am alive to enjoy them. Is there anything I can offer you, Mr. Kent? Tea?"

"Thank you," said Kent. "But I've just had lunch."

He reached into his pocket, but instead of taking out the letter, he pulled out his checkbook. "You would do me a great honor," he said simply, "if you would allow me to give you a small check."

Harry Summerfield raised both hands in a gesture of declining.

"You can pay me back," said Kent, "once your finances are straightened out."

Summerfield shook his head. "I have never been able to earn enough to save." He sounded almost ashamed. "With four children to feed, it just wasn't possible. My wife helped. She worked as a practical nurse, but even then ... And now? Maybe we shouldn't have had so many children. We came to this country penniless, but after what we'd been through..." He took a deep breath, as if what he was about to say took courage. "You see, Mr.

Kent, both my wife and I survived Dachau. Not our parents. Not our brothers and sisters. To us both our miraculous survival seemed like a command to give life, to replace what had been murdered." One big, single tear trickled from under the dark glasses, down the old man's cheek. He didn't wipe it away. "Can you understand? We came through it, crazy as this may sound, with a passion for life."

"And I must, I feel impelled to help you, in the only way I can," said Kent. "Please accept, for my sake," and he wrote the check. He was about to hand it to Summerfield when a voice cried from the kitchen, the voice that had told the dog to be quiet, "You're not going to accept money from that bastard?"

A third boy burst into the room. He was older than Walter or Eugene, a young man really. There was a strong resemblance between him and his father except that he wore a beard, a darker beard than his hair, which was a startling, flaming red.

"Stay out of this, Jacob," Summerfield said, trying to put some authority into the command. But Jacob grabbed the check out of Kent's hand, crushed it into a ball and threw it on the floor. Eugene immediately retrieved it, stuffed it into his pocket and rushed out the front door, slamming it shut after him.

"What do you mean, stay out of it?" cried Jacob. "I'm the oldest one, and with you in the condition you're in, I consider myself the head of the family, like it or not. To me this guy is a bastard. He crashed the plane we were on, and look at him. He survived. And now he has the gall to come here and feel sorry for us."

"The papers said he was not to blame," Walter got up angrily.

"The papers!" Jacob shouted. "Who's fool enough to believe what the papers say. This is a country of crooks." He turned on his father. "You should have gone to Israel instead of coming here."

"I did my best to bring the plane down safely," said Kent. "Every pilot does. Pilots don't want to die."

"But you survived. You'll get your job back, while

98

we . . . Here I am, in college, on scholarship, sure, but can I finish? No. I have to give it up, find a job. And you . . . you wouldn't have any idea what that means today. With two years of political science behind me, for what do I apply?"

"Maybe I can find you a job, Jacob," said Kent.

"And then I have to be grateful to you, who blinded my father and killed my mother and my sister?"

"You shouldn't have said that," said Walter.

Jacob struck his brother a vicious blow.

Harry Summerfield rose to his feet. He said with great dignity, "Did you hit your brother? I won't have fighting in my house, not as long as I'm alive. I've seen too much brute force to condone a stronger boy hitting a weaker one. Please leave the room. But first apologize to Mr. Kent."

"Apologize? I wish him the worst that could happen to him. He should lose his wife, his daughter, and his job." Then he actually spat and left the room.

"I feel I have to apologize for my son," said Mr. Summerfield, his voice filled with sorrow and embarrassment. "Please don't take him seriously, Mr. Kent. He can't seem to get over the fact that for the moment, college is out. He has always been a brilliant student and has hated any kind of menial work. It will do him no harm to have put up with it for a while. Our hardships, I have discovered, can ennoble us. If we survive. And Jacob will survive."

Kent got up. "I must be going." He took a visiting card out of his pocket and handed it to Walter. "Will you do something for me? Let me know how all of you are making out."

"Sure will," said Walter. "Thank you."

Summerfield was holding out his hand. Kent grasped it. "Thank you for coming."

Walter saw him to the elevator. At the front door Gene met him. "Hi, Mr. Kent. That's an awful lot of money you made that check out for. Are you sure you can afford it?"

"Quite sure."

Suddenly the boy embraced him, then ran as if the

devil were after him, back into the house. "Walter will take Dad to the bank tomorrow," he shouted. "Thanks ever so much."

Kent got into the next taxi that came by. He made his plane to Kennedy, but instead of letting Kitty know he had arrived, he phoned to say he was still in Philadelphia and wouldn't be home until the next morning. He called Bill Ward but couldn't reach him, neither at his office nor at home. He thought of telephoning Anna. She seemed to be the only person he wanted to talk to right then, but shrugged the temptation away. He went into the bar at the airport and sat there for a long time, drinking and thinking that he had to tell the F.B.I. that Jacob Summerfield would have to be watched.

18

"So he isn't coming home tonight," said Sam, when Kitty put down the receiver. "In that case I'll sleep over, as promised."

"And you should go to bed now." Kitty turned to Kate. Kate pulled a face. "You have a riding lesson tomorrow before school." Kitty had wanted to cancel the lessons, for which Kate had saved her money, babysitting, but hadn't dared. It might have made the child nervous.

Sam had shifted to a more comfortable position in the old rocking chair Kitty had bought at an auction, a beauty, with some of the old original stencil on the back slat. Something was sticking out from underneath his jacket.

"What's that?" asked Kate.

"My revolver." Sam took the gun out of his pocket and put it down on the table. "A Smith-Wesson thirty-eight."

"You always carry it with you?" asked Kate.

"Always."

"Why?"

"In times like these . . ." He smiled at her reassuringly. "Don't worry, I have a permit."

"And would you use it?"

"Sure would, if necessary."

"What if the other person shot first?"

"Wouldn't have much of a chance with me," said Sam.

Kent, Kitty thought, should have a gun. If he showed the letter to the police, he would certainly get a permit.

"I'd like to learn to shoot," said Kate. "Would you teach me, Sam?"

Kitty was suddenly just as interested. "Target-shooting, naturally," she said. "I couldn't kill anybody, I'm afraid.

I'm sure Kate couldn't, either."

"Oh, yes, I could," said Kate. "If anyone were to attack you, or Thomas, or me, I'd shoot."

"Now this is a hand-loading revolver," said Sam. He opened the safety-catch, showed them the loading chamber for six rounds, how to put in the bullets, snap the revolver shut and put the lock on safety again. Then he put the gun back in his pocket. "The history of firearms is really quite interesting," he said. "I don't know how much you know about it. The Chinese discovered gun powder as far back as the ninth century, but never did anything to develop firearms until the middle of the fourteenth, when most countries did. Actually firearms are the evolutionary product rather than the forerunners of the heavy ordnance.

"What's heavy ordnance?" asked Kate.

"Cannons," said Sam. "Somewhere around fourteen-fifty, a really revolutionary improvement in the handgun was made."

It was as good as impossible to stop Sam, once he'd started showing off his knowledge. He should have become a teacher, thought Kitty, but she found herself listening to his words with the same interest as Kate. "Then the first genuine matchblock was introduced," he went on. "The next elaboration was an improved lock mechanism. The Spanish latter produced a modification of the arquebus. It was radically different from the older types. The chief advantage over the lighter and more easily operable hand-cannon lay in the velocity and range. But the matchblock still suffered from various difficulties. It got damp too easily, and there were other snafus. The invention of the wheelblock helped, but it was complex and terribly expensive. Coincidental with that was the discovery of rifling."

"Meaning what?" Kate's eyes were shining with interest.

"Too long to explain. Besides, you're supposed to be off to bed. Anyway, experimentation went on throughout the centuries. The flintlock made for renewed interest. Only about a hundred and thirty years ago the ideal bullet was supplied by a French army captain and only ninety years ago, approximately, the Winchester, followed by the Remington, Marlin, Colt, and what have you, made history."

"If you're not a walking encyclopedia," said Kate. "And the way you remember it all. With me it just goes in one ear and out the other."

"Why don't you read up on it in the *Britannica* I gave you on your birthday three years ago? Read a couple of sentences, then repeat them backwards. You'll learn how something builds up and how to concentrate."

"And right now you're going to concentrate on going to bed," Kitty told Kate.

"Anyone want some ice cream?"

Kitty and Sam said thank you, no.

"May I take some to bed?"

"If you go at once."

After having planted a kiss on each of their foreheads, Kate finally left. Sam Slew stared after her. "How beautiful she is, and so graceful, and interested in almost everything."

"Strong, too," said Kitty. "I'm always surprised at the weight she can lift. Well, most of her interest right now lies in sports. Kent, of course, is all for it. Sometimes I think he brings her up too much like a boy."

As if he hadn't been listening, Sam went on. "But not as beautiful as you. I shall never forget the day I saw you again after not having seen you for ... God knows how many years. My last glimpse of you was a pretty girl, and then ... They were shooting some photos of you outside the Plaza. It was a bitter-cold day but you stood there in a bareback blue evening dress, shivering. I recognized you immediately."

"That was when I'd just started to work as a model," said Kitty. "I wasn't well known enough yet to be driven home, and when I was finally through and I'd changed and came out of the hotel with my little suitcase, there you were. And was I ever glad to see you! You took me home."

"I wanted to propose to you then and there," said Sam. "But I didn't feel I could until I'd made enough money to give you everything I wanted you to have."

"Is that why I saw so little of you? Because you felt you couldn't afford me? I wish you'd turned up more often. I was lonely at the time. I didn't have any friends in New York, and I certainly didn't care for the guys who took a pretty model out with only one thing in mind. And I felt safe with you. That goes way back, of course. But I do remember how you drove me out here and showed me a house you were working on, and how you said some day you'd be your own boss. And now you are. You're one of those rare persons who's realized his dream."

"Partially," said Sam. "But I wonder if you have any idea what a bitter-sweet assignment it was for me when you asked me to build your house, yours and Kent's."

"Of course I didn't," said Kitty. "How could I imagine that you were really serious about me? I don't think you really were, Sam."

"I can remember something you may not be able to recall. Kate was a year old, no — less, I think, because you were still feeding her. I walked in one day and there you sat feeding her, but instead of being embarrassed and leaving the room, you went right on, and I saw your breast, young and proud like an apple that had ripened in the sun."

"Sam!" Kitty's tone was sharp. "If I'd had any idea at the time that you were still in love with me, I certainly would have left the room. Now stop it."

"Don't worry," said Sam. "I've transferred all my feelings for you to Kate, who looks just like you when you were her age."

He poured himself a bourbon from the bottle in front of him, which Kitty had set out on a tray with only one glass. He held it out to her. She took it from him. "Just a sip."

"I suppose you've never been unfaithful to Kent?" he said abruptly, half statement, half question.

It caught her off balance. She could feel herself blush and hoped he wouldn't notice. "I used to be very old-fashioned," she said, avoiding a direct answer. "I didn't think it was right for a married couple to feel free to sleep with anyone else, even if they both did and didn't mind."

"And today?"

"Now," Kitty said slowly, "I sometimes think that a man and wife should be free to do whatever they want without it necessarily spoiling their relationship."

She took another sip of Sam's glass, a large one this time. He looked at her, surprised. He'd hardly ever seen her drink. At cocktail parties she usually hung onto a glass of water with a peel of lemon in it, pretending it was gin or vodka. "So you've changed," said Sam.

Kitty shook her head. "I don't think so. Not really. Just more tolerant, I guess."

Sam reached for the bottle. This time he took neither soda nor water, just a few pieces of ice. Then he said, "So you're not jealous of Anna any more."

"How can I be jealous of anybody who's been ruined as she has?"

"But you were."

Kitty shrugged. "What woman could help it? Anna is so much younger than I, so much more beautiful. And fascinating. But today . . ."

"But she's still in love with your husband, and he loves her."

"He feels pity for her."

"Are you sure that's all?"

"It's what he says."

"And you trust him?"

"That he wouldn't leave me for another woman — yes. If only because of Kate. He knows I'd fight for her, and since he would be the guilty party, I'd certainly get custody."

"So it's Kate that keeps you two married."

"Great God, no! There are other things. Many other things. Sex isn't the most important element in a marriage. Unless you're friends, it's no good."

"Maybe another man could arouse passion in you."

Kitty got up. She didn't want to think of Maximilian Forster and the way he made her feel, neither did she want to think of Anna and Kent making love. She turned on the radio. "Let's hear the news and then go to bed."

There were the usual dismal reports from all over the world. "Turn it off," said Sam. "It's too despressing. For the first time in my life I'm glad I don't have children. If I think what the children of today are going to have to cope with . . ."

"Every generation has to cope with tragedy. They'll manage. I want to hear the weather report. Kent's coming back tomorrow, and most accidents happen on a short trip."

"But it's June. No storms, no fog."

"I was never afraid before, though I encountered some rough moments as an airplane hostess. Flying to Peru one day . . ." she shivered. "But then I was young, with the feeling that nothing horrible could happen to me, and not dependent on someone I loved. But since the crash . . ."

They listened in silence to the usual things going on in Washington, in other countries. Then suddenly, in the same dull voice, the reporter announced that a man, a private detective, had been found strangled in his own car near Kennedy Airport. Bill Ward of Great Neck, Long Island. Three children had perished in a fire on Staten Island because of an exploding boiler in the bathroom, and an old lady had been mugged in a self-service elevator and was in serious condition at Bellevue.

"Did he say Bill Ward?" asked Kitty, her voice almost inaudible.

"I think he did." Sam was frowning. They dialed another station to try to get the news again, found one finally, and there it was, Bill Ward, private detective from Great Neck, Long Island.

Kitty began to cry.

"I didn't know you liked him that much," said Sam.

"It isn't that." Suddenly Kitty was furious. "Sam, you have no imagination. You never connect things. It doesn't occur to you that Bill Ward might have found the person who wrote that terrible letter, and was killed because he did. And now maybe we'll never know . . . or it'll be too late . . ."

She couldn't stop crying. Sam came slowly over to

where she sat on the couch. He held a full glass of bourbon out to her. She swallowed all of it.

"Don't cry," he said. "Please don't cry. After all, he's a detective and to find out who wrote the letter is certainly not his only job. There can be lots of other reasons why someone got him."

His logic made no impression on Kitty. She had not even listened to what he was saying, wrapped up as she was in her fear for Kate.

"I never believed he'd find the guy," she said, her voice a murmur, "but he must have."

"I'll see that nothing happens to Kate," said Sam. "I love her as if she were my own daughter. Even if I have to engage more help so as to have more time to keep an eye on her." He walked over to the French window that opened out onto the terrace, fingered the lock. "Tomorrow I'm going to have one of the boys put security locks on every door in the house," he said. Kitty shuddered. Sam came over, sat down beside her, put an arm around her shoulder. "Hush. Calm down." He stroked her hair, and she laid her head on his shoulder. "It will all come out all right," he said.

"I'm worried about Kent," Kitty whispered. "Now more than ever he'll pursue his crazy search for the writer of the letter. And he isn't even aware how idiotic that is. Ward told him, the F.B.I. told him it would be of no use. He's acting absolutely irrationally — oh, not on the outside — he pretends to laugh it off and I know it's not just for my sake or Kate's. But an attempt to keep his sanity. Oh, Sam, Sam, what's going to become of us all?"

19

Late sunday afternoon.

Kate usually loved to go for walks alone. There was in her the same kind of restlessness which at times plagued her mother. During the last few weeks, since the letter had come, she had almost never been alone. Not that they'd been obvious about it. She had to admit they had tried their best not to let her notice that for some reason or other somebody, quite often Sam, had been around when she wasn't at school. Even when she went over to see Anna, Kitty or Thomas would offer to drive her instead of letting her take her bicycle, which she preferred. And Anna would call when she was ready to leave, so that someone could pick her up. Jerry, too, seemed more attentive than before, though he never let on having been told not to let her out of his sight. They're afraid for me, thought Kate. Silly.

She called Zero. "Boy," she told him, "we're going for a walk. But first we're going to have ice cream cones." Zero liked ice cream just as much as she did. "And then we'll walk through the woods. The laurel's so lovely right now, and you and I haven't had nearly enough exercise lately. We're meeting Jerry and we'll try to outrace him."

They reached the park with its picnic grounds and tennis courts. There were paths through the woods, with a few people walking on them. Here she could let Zero off the leash, if she didn't have the bad luck to run into a cop.

Jerry wasn't there. She was rarely miffed, but today his failure to meet them as promised annoyed her. Since she had been twelve, almost three years ago now, she had liked him best of all the boys in the neighborhood, and he had been at her beck and call. Impatient, like her parents, she didn't feel like waiting. Of course he'd turn up eventually, with excuses for being late; his mother had wanted him to do an errand, or had insisted that he do his homework first. But she knew his mother was the permissive kind, and his father, a dentist, didn't particularly care what either his wife or his son did, as long as the former kept house for him the way he wanted it kept and Jerry didn't flunk out. Maybe he was practicing. He played the fiddle quite well, and hoped to be able to have his own band some day, not just play in the school band, which, both were agreed, was lousy. Well, to hell with him. If he didn't care enough about being with her to be on time, he'd soon lose her.

She started to walk slowly, then, when she was sure she was safe, she unleashed Zero. There were very few people in the woods, most of them home, she guessed, gardening or reading the Sunday papers. In a second Zero was gone, chasing a rabbit, probably, or maybe just excited by a falling leaf or a frog gurgling with sexual desire. Kate knew quite a bit about sex, having attended a modern school that exhibited plastic forms of the various organs. Also, some of her classmates had already had intercourse. Most of them were on the pill. And then, Thomas had carried her when she had still been quite little, into the shower, holding her tight in his arms, gradually getting her used to a stream of hot water, then cold, then warm again, cold again, then tepid. She had noticed that he had something she didn't have, and that he used it when he went to the john, and for months she had tried in vain to pinch her tiny vagina together so that she could do it like him. It had never been a success. But she had asked what that thing was that hung out on two balls, and he had told her it was a male member, a phallus through which passed the sperm that might impregnate the ovaries of a woman, and then, if everything went all right, she could have a child. She had asked a lot of questions and he had answered them scientifically. In Sweden, Kate had read somewhere, little girls only ten years old were soliciting on street corners, and she was sorry for them. She couldn't imagine that she would enjoy

Jerry sticking what he called his prick into her. The expression in itself was somehow repulsive. He had, of course, called her silly, and mentioned the names of girls in her class who didn't mind but thought it was fun. Good for them, but she didn't want it yet. Not from a boy who was just a couple of years older than she, and didn't know much more than she did, except for the fact that he got a great kick out of 'laying a girl'. He had called her a sissy and a no good sport. To hell with him. Her boy would have to look a lot like her father, behave like him, gentle but with authority, yet have respect for her feelings. And if she didn't want any more, that was that. She had an absolute horror of a girl in her class, Melanie, who always wanted to be close to her, carry her books, help her in any way she could, and in the locker room to touch her breasts.

Kate kept her eyes on the ground, intent on finding some mushrooms. She didn't like the champignons Mom grew on little shelves in the cellar. She preferred the pfifferlings in cans, a lovely reddish brown, with long stems and a funny, frizzy umbrella on top. Lately they had gone up in price and been scarce. There were some mushrooms around, in certain neighborhoods, that looked very much like them but were poisonous, and anyway, she was a good half hour away from anywhere where she might find edible mushrooms. It was plain silly to look for any here.

She heard a sound behind her, a sound of running feet. Jerry? But Jerry would have called out, "Hi, Kate. Wait," and caught up with her breathlessly, his toe sticking out of his right sneaker where he'd torn it. There was no such call. Maybe it was just somebody exercising.

Kate whistled, but Zero didn't appear. Suddenly there was no doubt in her mind — somebody was following her. I should have turned around long ago to see who it is, Kate told herself. Why didn't I? She began to walk faster; whoever was following her walked faster too. He was breathing heavily, an almost labored sound, as if whoever it was wasn't used to physical exercise.

Kate swung around sharply and came face to face with

a boy, older than she but lightweight. Redhaired, with a red beard. It was by instinct rather than by a conscious reflex that Kate fell back on one of the first defenses she had learned in judo. She took a step forward, got hold of the boy's right arm behind the elbow and with her right hand grabbed his lapel. With a quick shove and a tug she pushed his weight back onto his right leg and simultaneously swept her right foot forward, then back, catching his right leg and kicking it out from under him. The entire action took only a second or two. He fell on his back with a grunt. Kate started to run, but he got up fast, caught up with her, grabbed her by the shoulder, threw her to the ground and himself on top of her. She could see him reach for a knife in his trouser pocket. A gleam of sunlight hit the blade, making it look like pure, shiny silver, and then the meaning of the knife hit her. She screamed.

And Zero was there, like an apparition. The boy, or man, didn't notice him, had perhaps never realized that she had a dog with her. With one of his mighty leaps, Zero attacked the redheaded boy from the back. His powerful jaws dug into the boy's shoulder, tearing it, tearing his weight away from Kate. He rolled over, moaning, and lay there, the blood pouring from his shoulder. Still Zero wouldn't let go. He clawed at the boy's back, he bit him in the leg, parrying every move his mistress' attacker made to drive him off. "Let go, Zero! Let go!" Kate yelled. She had to repeat the command several times before Zero finally obeyed.

"Home," Kate told him, without looking back. Zero didn't need to be leashed. He heeled, looking up at her balefully, yet at the same time proudly.

"Good dog," Kate told him, "good dog," and leaned down to stroke him.

Her legs were shaking, and a little farther on, knowing that there was no danger of her attacker following them, she stopped to do some exercises, moving her legs rhythmically, breathing deeply in and out, her arms above her head, lowering them, raising them again. After that, her body felt lighter, but her heart was still thumping.

For a while she walked slowly, holding onto Zero's collar. She had leashed him again, and for once he didn't seem to resent being tied, as if he wanted to be a part of her.

Thomas was sitting at the swimming pool, writing. Kitty had wanted to cancel an invitation to play bridge with the Travers, a family who had moved into their neighborhood a couple of weeks ago, but he had urged her to go because he thought it would distract her.

"Where in God's name were you?" he called out to Kate. "Jerry came by, desperate. You told us you were going for a walk with him."

"He didn't turn up in time."

"Will you never learn to wait, at least five minutes?"

"I don't see why I should," said Kate.

"And where are you going now?"

"To feed Zero."

She went into the kitchen, opened the refrigerator but found nothing good enough to reward him. Then the lovely smell of roast beef in the oven hit her nose. She took it out. Not done enough yet. Beef was expensive, still she cut off a hunk, sliced it into sizeable pieces and put them in Zero's bowl. Her share, if Mom complained. She didn't feel like eating anyway.

"Kate!"

Kate stuck her head out the back door. "If you don't mind, Thomas, I'm terribly tired. I ... I think I'll go straight to bed."

"In the afternoon? You aren't coming down with anything? Do you have a temperature?"

"I've got cramps. Just the usual. I'll take Mydol and sleep it off."

Zero, having finished his elaborate dinner in a few gulps, followed her upstairs. He sat next to the bathtub, watched her soak, and waited for her to hang a leg over the edge so he could lick it. "Good old Zero," Kate told him. "But we won't let Thomas or Mom know, will we? There's some blood on you. Here, hold still, I'll wash it off."

The blood of a stranger, of a red-haired, red-bearded boy. Well, maybe he hadn't meant any harm, just a joke to frighten an attractive girl whom he might have wanted to screw. "Screw," Kate said aloud. It was such a funny expression. But no, there had been the knife, gleaming silver in the sunlight. She shuddered.

She fetched a glass of milk and got into bed. She took one of her favorite books from the shelf, then put it back and reached for the encyclopedia. Volume with F. Firearms. She read all about them. It sounded more complicated than when Sam had reeled it off. She would get Kitty to agree that he teach them to shoot. When she heard Thomas' steps coming up the stairs, she closed her eyes, pretending to be asleep, so did Zero. He lay at the foot of Kate's bed, soundlessly, his beautiful head with the white streak on the forehead buried between his paws. Motionless. Just the ears twitching now and then. Thomas Kent closed the door softly.

20

"BILL WARD IS dead," Kent told Anna. "Murdered is what the papers say."

"I know. I heard it over the radio. And of course all of us are thinking that possibly he tracked down the person or someone connected with the threatening letter."

They were sitting on the small terrace in front of her living room, Anna, wearing her artificial limb, Kent with his cane leaning next to the lounge chair he was sitting in. Anna's father had left a few days ago, much against his will but seeming somehow relieved. Inside the house was an elderly woman Anna had found to live with her for board and lodging and a small weekly salary — a Mrs. Rogers.

"When did you see Gordon last?" Kent asked.

Anna leaned forward to pour some fruit juice Mrs. Rogers had fixed and placed between them in a pitcher on the white, painted iron table with the flowery sun umbrella in the middle. "A few days ago," she said. "You're not jealous of him by any chance?"

"Perhaps. In a way."

"What way?"

"There are as many jealousies in life as there are different flowers or trees or animals."

"He's a very entertaining man."

"And I'm not?"

Anna didn't answer the question but went on. "He has a wonderfully perceptive mind."

"How did you meet him?"

"I was with the Concert Company. I was dancing the Queen of the Wilis in Giselle for the first time. He was down front, and next day there were roses. A huge bunch. Red ones. No note, just a card. And during the last week we were in New York, there was a letter about how much he admired me, and a touching bit about his being so alone. His wife had died many years ago. And would I do him the honor to have dinner with him one evening, whenever it suited me. And his telephone number. The night before we left New York, I called him."

Kent looked surprised. "I wouldn't have thought you would."

Anna laughed. "Kent, darling, haven't you found out yet that I like men, that I need sex? I know people say dancers can't fit it in, but I've always been able to. Why are you suddenly interested in him?"

"Because I'd like to meet him."

"What for?"

"Quite apart from my determination to see every one of the survivors, I've got another reason. The tree doctor who took a look at the willow next to our swimming pool told me he had been at Gordon's place this morning, and a red-haired, red-bearded boy had been trimming some branches off a tree." He still couldn't get over the fact that the F.B.I. hadn't informed him that Gordon had engaged a boy who might quite well be Harry Summerfield's oldest son. Evidently they had paid no attention to his warning. "I have a hunch he may be Jacob Summerfield."

"But you can't suspect every red-haired boy . . ."

"You're right, but for various reasons I don't want to go into, I'd like to see that boy."

"I don't think Gordon will want to see you. He sees very few people, and you'd only remind him of the tragedy."

"Do me the favor," said Kent. "Please. Call him and tell him you're coming over for a short visit or whatever you want to use as an excuse. I'll drive you over and stay in the car. I'm sure you can manage to get him to see me for a few minutes. It's very important to me."

"Oh, Thomas." A tone almost of anger colored her voice. "You know I can't resist you. I do whatever you want, even when you're taking advantage of me. It makes me furious to think you can ask anything of me, and like a fool, I'll do it. What is it about you that makes people want to do anything for you?"

She got up and went into the house. She's really learning how to walk gracefully with that contraption, thought Kent. A few minutes later she came back, a kerchief around her head from under which her black curls fell to her shoulders. "All right."

They drove away from King's Point towards Seacliff; later Anna directed him onto a narrow back lane. After about two miles she pointed out a big blue boulder at the side of the road which Kent would have overlooked. The name "Gordon" was painted on it in white. There was no gate, only an opening wide enough for cars to pass through. They drove along a magnificent driveway bordered by apple trees, then through a stand of elms behind which the green of fir trees looked like a dark sea. It led to a circle which they rounded and arrived at a high stone wall with a small gate, also painted blue. At each side dogs were tied on long chains, Dobermans. Their coats almost blue with red markings. They stood a little more than two feet and weighed, Kent guessed, around seventy pounds. Their well-knit bodies were a sight to behold.

"I don't like them," said Kent. "They've such vicious character. I always wondered about the man after whom they're called and what kind of a guy he was."

"Gordon is very proud of them," Anne told him, "and they really are excellent watchdogs. Blow your horn, Thomas."

He did, and a white uniformed servant appeared, took the dogs and led them out of sight, after which he came back to help Anna out of the car. He paid no attention to the man who was driving her.

Anna walked through the little blue gate and came back five minutes later. "I couldn't make up a story," she said. "I had to tell him you were here and wanted to see him. Follow me."

At the end of a small path, on both sides of it beds filled with exotic flowers, there was another opening, this time between a hedge cut to seven feet high. Kent stood, holding his breath. He had seen many beautiful landscapes but this one was so unexpectedly lovely, he couldn't take it in all at once. Meadows stretched out before him, acres of them, the land falling gradually toward a small stream with high trees sheltering it from the road. On the hilly ground on which he stood, an outsize swimming pool mirrored the sky, its blue intensified by chemicals. On the canvas-shaded terrace, a man sat in a wheelchair. He wore no shirt and his chest showed a deep mahogany tan, so did his face. Fifty years old at the most, thought Kent, in spite of the deep furrows around his powerful chin. His hair was iron grey above a rather broad, low forehead, his eyes an almost unbelievable forget-me-not blue. They seemed to see straight through Kent.

"It is very good of you to see me," Kent bowed.

"I didn't want to," said Gilbert Gordon, his voice a melodious bass. "But Anna can make any man do whatever she wants. Sit down. What can I offer you?"

"Iced coffee," Anna answered. "With plenty of whipped cream on the top and a straw, and maybe just a touch of brandy to give it more taste. No, not Irish coffee, but as cold as can be."

"And for you, Mr. Kent?"

"The same, please."

Gilbert Gordon gave the order. There must have been an intercom which relayed every word spoken on the terrace to the kitchen. The coffee appeared, served in tall glasses on an elaborate silver tray. There was none for Gordon, who helped himself to some water from a silver ewer. Next to his chair stood two telephones. Both rang almost simultaneously. He picked one up, put the other on hold, "Excuse me." He spoke quickly and sharply to one of his callers, at greater length to the other. "No, I am unable to give you any advice. I simply don't know. If anyone tells you he does, don't believe him. We've never had to cope with things quite as they are at present, and anybody who is sure he can make a profit for you is a fool. Talk to you tomorrow."

Watching him, listening to him, Kent knew that any

suspicion of Gordon was ridiculous. He turned to Kent. "Now I am sure you didn't ask Anna to drive you up here to ask my advice on what to do with your investments."

"Don't be mean, Bertie." Anna put her hand on his. "I told you he wanted to show you a letter, and . . ."

"So, where is it?"

Kent hesitated. "It's really not necessary any longer," he said, "I'd much rather have your permission . . ."

But Gordon interrupted him. "I want to see it. Where is it?"

Kent handed Gordon the letter and the man read it with what seemed to Kent a mere glance. "The worst," he said, "is the instinct of cruelty with a good conscience which is a delight to moralists. I don't always agree with Russell but . . ." he shrugged. Then handed the letter back to Kent. "Why did you want to show it to me?"

"I wanted to ask you if you had any idea who could possibly have written the letter."

"No, you didn't. You wanted to form an opinion as to whether *I* could possibly have written it."

Against his will, Kent nodded. "Out of the question, of course, though I think you are a man of strong feelings, ruthless if you have to be."

"Oh, Kent," whispered Anna.

Gordon turned to face her. "Darling, don't you know yet that I can't be offended except sometimes by my own actions?" He reached for her hand and pressed it to his lips. Then he turned to Kent again. "You are quite right — ruthless when I have to be, and then again, at times, hopelessly sentimental. I imagine you're wondering — do I blame you or hate you? Well, there are hours when I do both. Some years ago I lost a lovely daughter, and what that does to a father I am sure you will understand, since you have a lovely daughter yourself. All I have left is a no-good son. Right now I don't even know where he is. I loved my wife. My daughter was very much like her and this sometimes gave me the illusion that she was still alive. Then she too was gone." He took a deep breath and went on, almost drily. "Then I found Anna, and she seemed to epitomize everything I had lost." He looked at Kent intently. "And you see what the crash did to her. I shall walk again, so I have been told, certainly I shall be mobile enough for every purpose in my life. But Anna . . . Yes, I could have written that letter. At night, in the dark, when you can't sleep and are too tired to read, armies of crazy thoughts assail you. There were nights when I could gladly have wrung your neck, nights when I wanted you to suffer some of the agony all of us were suffering." He paused. Suddenly he looked old.

"Do you still feel that way about me?"

"I always forget things I don't like about myself."

"A very wise attitude," said Kent. "I wish I could make it mine. But wanting to meet you was the least of my reasons. Something much more important made me ask Anna to bring me here. I heard you engaged a boy recently to work in the garden, a red-haired, red-bearded boy. I'd appreciate it if I could have a few words with him."

Gordon pressed a bell and within seconds his man servant appeared. "Has the new boy left," Gordon asked him, "or is he still around?"

"He left last night, sir."

Gordon turned to Kent. "Sorry."

"Would you be so good as to tell me his name and what kind of impression you had of him?"

For just a second Gordon looked startled, and Kent felt obliged to explain. "I went to see a family called Summerfield in Philadelphia — among the survivors was a boy who struck me as hysterical and revengeful — blaming me for the crash. Jacob Summerfield."

"Sorry, I don't recall his name. Just Jay. My secretary will. Anyhow, a strange young man. He answered my ad for a gardener's helper. He'd had a summer job on a farm, he said in his application." He paused, went on. "If I remember correctly, from the moment I laid eyes on him I knew he wasn't interested in gardening or animals, and he certainly knew nothing about either. What he really wanted to learn about was money. A chance for a job in my office. I told him not to bother me, that it was out of the question for someone with none of the knowledge required, but I couldn't shake him off. He was always around, always hinting that he and I had something in common. No idea what he meant, but I soon got the impression that he was mentally disturbed. Would have had to get rid of him anyway, but then he got himself into a bloody mess, and I mean bloody. Some dog attacked him. Not any of mine, I'm glad to say. Well, he's gone. Disappeared."

"Do you happen to know where?"

Anna's eyes, filled with compassion, were resting on Kent. Gordon, apparently noticing her glance, said slowly, "No idea. And now, Mr. Kent, I think you have all the information you wanted, consciously or subconsciously."

Kent rose. "Thank you for seeing me."

Anna remained seated. "Don't worry about Anna," said Gordon. "I'll get her home whenever she's bored with me."

Kent tried to catch her eye, but she was watching a silvery canoe coming up the stream below them. He bowed and walked to his car. As he left, the dogs barked furiously.

21

BILL WARD IS dead. They found him strangled in his car. Murdered. I wonder who could be behind that. Probably he forgot to settle one of his debts and they got tired of waiting, or he hired some hoods to raid the place where he gambled, and they got him. In a way I'm sorry he died. Not exactly because he's dead. We were never friends. But when I think how he died — I could vomit. Possibly too sure of himself — he was arrogant in his vulgar way — didn't think any harm could come to him when a couple of guys offered him a ride. I suppose one sat next to him, the other in the back. And the one in the back suddenly slung a wire noose around his neck. That's what the paper said. Garroted. I guess he had it coming to him. But I want to die in my sleep. Preferably a heart attack, and that just might be it. Because last time I had a check-up, the doctor told me I had a murmur, and my cardiogram wasn't all it should be. He showed it to me, tried to explain the irregularities in the graph, and warned me to take it easy. Which is what I'm doing. But I must admit, the fact that Thomas Kent is still alive distresses me. It's weeks now since he got my letter. His mind is uneasy, I'm sure of that. But the fact that he's worried isn't enough. I want him dead.

I shouldn't really be so eager to see him dead. For a few weeks his anxiety will be the kind of torture I'm happy to inflict on him. A clear sudden death would be easier than having to live with the constant fear that something might happen to Kate. So, as I see it now, I shouldn't be all that impatient. What I did to that wild dog I'm doing to him in a way. Do I enjoy seeing him suffer? Lord, yes. I do. Just as I enjoyed making that dog suffer. Just as the boys hanging me upside down over the john must have enjoyed hearing me moan. But they were too cowardly to watch me. They closed the door and stayed outside, listening to my muffled screams. Did they close the door to frighten me more or didn't they have the guts to watch the blood making my face swell? I'll never know. One of the guards saved me, but when he asked who'd done it, I didn't give them away. I knew the names of every one of them, but I could think of better ways to revenge myself. Oh, I'm a great one for revenge. Revenge is sweet. As far as I'm concerned, it's the most satisfying feeling in the world. But I never did revenge myself on them. A mistake. Maybe if I had, I wouldn't have had to revenge myself on Kent. I know when I realized I had to for the first time — it was the night of the crash, and shapeless bodies of the dead lying on the snow. I saw my dead sheep again.

But this endless searching for a justification is boring. I want him dead, and that's that, whatever the reason. Meanwhile, it's satisfying to create an even deeper hysteria in his mind, which might influence his judgment in flying. Next time he might not get away with just a few broken bones. What do I care about the other people? Not a damn, if you really want to know. But if I could create a genuine derangement in his mental capacities, it would serve my purpose just as well. I think I shall send him another letter.

22

THERE WAS DEFINITELY a new element between them in bed. Kent was more considerate, or perhaps you could call it sensitive, and Kitty was ready to do things he had longed for but never demanded of her. But what had surprised Kitty most, the evening she had come back from New York after her afternoon with Max, was that after only a slight hesitation, she was ready to sleep with Kent. Two men in one day? It frightened her. What am I turning into, she wondered? A whore? A woman to whom it doesn't matter with whom she's sleeping? A cheat? Even enjoying the knowledge that he doesn't know that a few hours ago I was with another man? No, that's not exactly true. I feel — well, not exactly guilty, but . . .

Kent wasn't used to her almost immediate response. It had always intrigued him that she had had to be "warmed up," as he had called it teasingly. Once he had compared her to one of those engines that had to be cajoled before they would react. "Kitty," he said, "have you been sleeping with somebody else?"

"You wouldn't tell me about your affairs. Why then do you ask me?"

"A man and a woman are different."

"Christ, Kent," said Kitty, "don't make me feel you were born a century ago."

"A century ago men and women were as different as when the world was created, and they still are."

Kitty shrugged. "You're incorrigible."

"Maybe I am. But I don't want to spoil our relationship."

"Nothing will spoil it. Nothing. You're the only man I truly love."

"I have to possess somebody I love, wholly. It's part

of my need, to feel sure that there is a human being, a woman you love and respect, who is entirely yours."

"And you think women don't feel that way? That women don't resent it when they think their man is doing the same thing with other girls? That they don't ask themselves, why can't they suffice? That they don't get inferiority complexes?"

"There was never anyone who could touch you in human values."

"But more fun?"

"Fun is the wrong word. A challenge, perhaps. Sex is the hunger and the food, oblivion and awareness, distraction and concentration, you and not you. The partner is a necessity, a toy, a prop, a loneliness shared and abused, excitement and illusion, the dream and the hard truth, sometimes holding those in love with each other in bondage."

"And I was no longer a challenge."

"When you weren't there."

"Oh, don't lie."

"I never had affairs, one-night stands, if you want to call them that."

"And what about Anna?"

Kent didn't answer.

"It's not that I'm pissed off about her," said Kitty.

Kent made a small movement of surprise. Kitty rarely used vulgar language. He moved away from her, to lie on his back, and she wondered if perhaps it wasn't just that. She wanted to prove to herself that she was just as good as a temperamental Polish girl, and assured by new knowledge, wanted to startle him, to feel more passionately desired.

"It's all because of that letter," she said, reaching for his hand.

"I don't think so," said Kent. "Maybe with me, but not with you. I think it started a while ago."

"What started a while ago?"

"Your being bored."

"Bored? Not with you, but with our life out here — yes. So often alone, waiting for you. Sometimes afraid of an accident. Getting up at a set hour to drive Kate to school, cleaning the house, fetching her home, driving her to dancing lessons, riding lessons, watching over her homework, shopping, cooking. And then the long evenings, alone with radio or television, letting Zero out, letting Zero in. Don't you think other women out here get bored? Why do you think so many of them sleep around?"

He knew her too well not to realize that her outburst, her sudden discontent, was her way of trying to put the blame on the life they had to live because they didn't want to raise Kate in the city. It was all part of their mutual fear.

"I wasn't talking about that kind of boredom. I was asking you when did you get bored sleeping with me?"

Was there a change in her since Max had roused her? Was Kent so sensitive as to notice a minute difference in her response? Or had the letter made him feel so helpless that he had begun to doubt himself as a male?

"Bored isn't the right expression. It's become routine. Just like taking a bath, a nice hot bath which you enjoy, always have enjoyed, but it's always the same. For you, too, I'm sure."

"So you broke it."

"Kent," she said, "you can't blame me if I did or if I didn't. It's all too much for me. I mean, this terror that's been imposed on us."

"I'm not blaming you. I understand. I don't want to know with whom you've been trying to escape. I just want us to stay together."

"But, Kent, can't you see what I'm going through? I either have to lose you or my daughter."

"You overlook the third and most important aspect," said Kent. "We have to find the person who wrote that letter. And we will."

He turned out the light. Both pretended to be asleep. So did Kate, who had heard most of the conversation, sitting on the window seat, listening to the sounds of the night. The best thing I could do, she thought, is drown myself. Then they wouldn't have to worry about me anymore. Maybe I will.

125

23

IN THE FIRST grey light of morning, Kate was awakened by a strange noise. It wasn't loud, and it seemed to come from close by. She got out of bed and tiptoed into Kent's room. He was lying quietly on his right side, no nightmares, no moan came from his lips. Kent always slept with the shades up, and Kate looked at her father, a lump in her throat. He seemed so much younger asleep, so much more vulnerable, almost like a boy. She wanted to get close to him, crawl into his bed, snuggle up against his warmth as she had been allowed to do when bad dreams had plagued her, until Kitty had put a stop to it a few years ago. "You can climb into my bed," she had told her, "any time you feel lonesome or troubled." And that had been that. If Kitty said something, she meant it. Then it struck Kate that Zero wasn't lying at the foot of Thomas' bed as usual.

She walked through the open door into her mother's room. Kitty, too, seemed to be sleeping peacefully, her pillows, her covers not disarranged. But Zero wasn't in Kitty's room either.

Tiptoeing through the house, she came to the kitchen, opened the back door, and heard the moan quite clearly. It came from the direction of the swimming pool. The dew was heavy and her feet got wet, but she didn't notice it.

Zero was lying on the flagstones near the rim of the pool, as if he had tried to reach it to drink the water. A thing he never did, knowing very well, after his first try, that the chemicals in it gave him a stomach ache and made him itch. She knelt down beside him. "Zero! What's the matter with you?"

She tried to stroke him. He almost snapped at her, a

126

mere attempt, because he could scarcely lift his head. The next minute he stuck out his tongue and licked her hand, as if he wanted to apologize. Then he quivered — it shook his entire body — and sank back, exhausted.

"Zero, look at me," Kate begged, her hand on his stomach.

He moaned again, but he opened his eyes and looked at her with glazed pupils, then shut them again.

Kate rushed back to the house. She took some milk from the icebox, warmed it and put it into a bowl. Should she use ice? What was better for convulsions? She decided on warmth, held a kitchen towel under the hot water, wrung it out, paying no attention to the way it burned her hands. She carried the luke warm milk and the hot towel to the swimming pool, put the hot towel on Zero's stomach, held the bowl to his mouth. Hardly lifting his head, he took a sip, but seemed to have difficulty in swallowing. Kate dipped her finger into the bowl, wetted his mouth, pressed the towel to his stomach. Zero went into convulsions again.

He's eaten something, she thought. Poison. Or maybe he fought a diseased cat. But there was no blood, no scar, no sign of scratches on him. She rushed up into the bathroom, got a Donatal, dissolved it in tepid water, went back to him, forced it down his throat. He spat it out. Now his whole body was twitching. He was sick, deathly sick. Who to get for help? Sam? She hated to wake him. He'd looked tired lately. Jerry? She'd probably get his father, who'd give her hell. Wake Thomas? He needed his rest. Kitty? She was so edgy lately. Call the vet? Of course. He'd charge an enormous fee to come over at this unearthly hour, but he was the best man around, a German refugee, a count who had left Germany on principle. She called him, Count Werder in Great Neck. "It's urgent. You've got to come right away. My dog is dying. No, 1 can't possibly move him. You've got to come."

She hated to leave Zero alone, but she had to open the gate for Werder to drive in. Since the letter it was kept closed at night. Thomas and Kitty — they were nervous, no doubt about it. As she walked to the gate, she found a piece of red meat in the driveway. She picked it up and put it into the pocket of her robe.

Werder arrived in less time than she had expected. He came from an old Bavarian family, but he looked more Jewish than any Jew she had ever known. A high forehead that seemed to fly back like a buttress from the root of his nose to his biocephally shaped pate. His nose was crooked, double-crooked, first at the root, then again in the middle, like a camel with two humps, a dromedary. He examined Zero with knowing hands. The muscles in the neck were stiff, yet twitching. He took Zero's temperature. It was high, so was his blood pressure. He was breathing as if he were suffocating. Then he had another convulsion. Tetanic convulsions, Werder thought. An immediate evacuation of the dog's stomach was imperative. "Poisoned, undoubtedly."

"He was all right at ten, when I went to bed. Thomas let him out, he always does before we turn in for the night." She showed him the piece of red meat she had found. Werder took it. "I'll have it examined. Strychnine or arsenic...in any case a powerful dose. We may be too late." He searched in his bag for some chloroform to allay Zero's spasms. "I'll want a blood test."

"Whatever's necessary. How long will it take before we know?"

"Half a day. A day. Depends on how busy they are at the lab."

"You can't do it yourself?"

Count Werder shook his head. "Don't have the equipment. Sorry."

"And in the meantime?"

"He'll suffer. Not for long, though, I'm afraid."

"I don't want him to suffer."

Werder looked at Zero quietly for a while, then he said, "I'd say it was strychnine. The question is how much of it got into him, and when he ate it."

"Strychnine? Then there's no hope for him, is there? Just more suffering."

"I'm afraid so. We do have some stuff that might..."

128

"And might not?"

"That's right. I'd like to give you some hope but . . . You're going to have to help me get him into my car."

Zero moaned again; he went into another convulsion, then lay still. "Put him out of his misery," said Kate.

"But you love him."

"That's why."

Count Werder reached into his little black bag, took out a hypodermic, filled it from a vial, squirted a few drops into the air, said, "Go away."

"No. I'll hold him."

"He might bite you."

"He won't," said Kate.

She walked around Zero's twitching body, knelt, and cradled his head in her hands. "Except for Thomas, I've always loved you best," she told him, and to the vet, "Go ahead."

Zero didn't bite, instead he stuck out the tip of his tongue to lick one of Kate's hands. A last violent convulsion and he didn't move any more.

"You're sure he's dead?"

"Positive."

"Have the meat examined and let me know. And send me the bill. Thank you for coming so fast. You're sure we've done the right thing?"

"Quite sure." Count Werder rose.

"Don't race the motor when you leave. My parents are still asleep, and there's no need to wake them now. Goodbye, and thanks again."

She sat for a long time next to the motionless body of her best friend. She didn't dare to touch him. Death was still a noble state for her, with which no one should interfere. At about five she finally rose from her hunched position and went into the kitchen. She dialed Jerry's number, and after a while a sleepy voice answered, "Who the hell . . ."

"I'm very sorry to wake you, Dr. Armstrong. It's Kate. Kate Kent. I've got to speak to Jerry. It's very important."

Something in her voice must have made Armstrong feel this wasn't just a teenage lack of consideration, for the next voice was Jerry's. "Get over here," she told him, "and help me dig a grave. And don't talk to me while we're doing it. Don't talk to me at all, or I'll kill you."

She had already started to loosen the soil under the red beech, which had been Zero's favorite tree. He had lain for hours under its shade. A second spade leaned against it.

"Jesus, this is terrible. What happened?"

"I told you not to talk to me. Get on with it."

It took them a good half hour to dig a hole wide and deep enough to lift Zero in and cover him. Then Kate trampled the disturbed ground flat by jumping on it.

"Go away now, Jerry. And thank you."

Jerry did as he was told, shaking his head, taking the two spades with him to put them in their place. Then he went back to Kate, who stood leaning against the tree. "I think you're terrific," he said.

"I wish you were Zero," Kate said.

Jerry, embarrassed by such genuine grief, barked. Kate slapped his face and Jerry stepped back, dismayed by the fury he had generated. Then he went away, a seventeen year old boy who didn't always know when to say the right thing.

After he had gone, Kate threw off her robe, her short nightgown, and dived into the pool. It was still cold at this early morning hour, when the sun had had no chance to warm it. She didn't know how long she swam; she got out only when she suddenly felt dizzy. She went straight back to bed, huddling under her comforter. To her surprise she found she couldn't cry.

24

As USUAL, KENT went into Kate's room to wake her for school. She was fast asleep, but there were tears below her closed lids. Kent stared at them disbelievingly. He had hardly ever been so deeply touched, as by seeing his daughter cry in her sleep. Nor was he used to seeing Kate cry. She had always been unable to give in to sorrow with tears. He touched her shoulder gently. "Time to get up, darling."

Kate pulled away from him and turned over on her stomach.

"You'll be late for school if you don't get up."

Kate sat up abruptly. "I'm not going to school today. I'm not going tomorrow either. I'm not going the whole week." She moved to the other side of the wide bed, out of his reach.

"Why? Don't you feel well? I think I'd better call the doctor."

"No doctor can help me." Kate's voice was monotonous. "I just want to be left alone. I want to die."

Kent sat down on her bed. "Would you please tell me what's the matter with you."

Kate turned around. In a cold, factual voice she said, "You might as well know. Zero is dead."

"Zero dead? You've had a nightmare, darling."

"Call the vet if you don't believe me. He was here, around four o'clock, and he thought it was strychnine poisoning, I mean what Zero died of. He's got the piece of meat I found in the driveway, and he's going to have it examined." All of a sudden she flung both arms around Kent's neck, and he could feel her body shaking with sobs. For a while he was unable to speak. Not only did he know what the dog meant to Kate, but the implications of what she had just told him struck him like a blow. Mechanically he stroked her shoulders. Frail bones under a silky, tanned skin.

"I'll get you another dog," he said finally, and Kate told him not to be assinine. "I don't ever want another dog. You think it's that easy to give your love to someone else? How do you think I'd feel if somebody offered me another father?" She pushed him away, feeling misunderstood for the first time by the person she loved and trusted most.

Kent went to his "cage" and called the vet. Count Werder confirmed what Kate had told him. "I could see at once that it was too late. Strychnine usually kills within twenty minutes."

When and why had Zero got out of the house? Had he heard a noise? Kent had taught the dog how to unbolt the kitchen door; he'd done so several times when he'd wanted to go out in the night. So it would have been quite possible for him to go after any sound that worried him, smelling along the path to the gate, picking up the meat that had been left there to kill him. Why would anyone want to kill Zero? The answer was obvious. Zero protected Kate.

Kent went down to the kitchen and made a cup of tea for Kitty, poured some instant coffee into a mug with boiling water for himself and brought up a glass of cold milk for Kate. She liked to start her day like that, before she had her oatmeal. He sat down on her bed again and held the glass of milk out to her. She shook her head. "Okay," he said. "And you don't have to go to school if you don't want to. Maybe the two of us can go for a long drive."

"I don't want to go for a drive. I buried Zero under the red beech. Jerry helped me. He's the most foolish boy I've ever known. You know what I want, Thomas? I want Mr. Hulbert to come over, all dressed up in his robes, and read something over Zero's grave. I don't want a marker on it, a cross, nothing like that. I couldn't stand a sign saying 'Here lies Zero, the most faithful and courageous dog that ever existed.' There are some beautiful psalms, and I'll find one that fits him. Do you think Mr. Hulbert would do it? For a dog?"

Kent, who hadn't known that Kate believed in Christian traditions, assured her that the minister would.

132

"And he saved my life."

"What do you mean — he saved your life?"

Kate looked at her father's drawn face. "Oh, you know, when I almost got run over two years ago. He ran between me and the car. His front leg was in a cast for weeks. Don't you remember? We talked about having him put away if his leg should remain stiff. And that night when I felt dizzy in the bathtub, just before my appendix ruptured — he pulled me up by the hair and ran downstairs, into the living room, barking madly to get your attention."

Kent remembered, but he knew that Kate had meant to tell something different, knew she was lying because her lips were trembling, and she reddened. Kate could never lie without blushing. Oh, Christ, he thought, fuck that letter and what it does to us. Making Kate lie.

"Kate," he said, "you're lying. You just told me Zero saved your life, but it has nothing to do with things long past. Now tell me the truth."

Kate sat up suddenly, as if his demand had finally cleared away her grief about Zero. "He did it," she said. "I'm sure he did it. He poisoned Zero."

"He? Who?"

"The red-haired boy who attacked me."

"Attacked you? When? Why didn't you tell me about it?"

"Didn't want to worry you. Didn't want to think about it. Wanted to forget it." Kate shuddered. "That Sunday afternoon in the woods . . . when Jerry wasn't there on time. Zero and I . . . if it hadn't been for Zero, I might be dead by now."

"What exactly happened?" Kent asked evenly.

"Zero and I went off alone and, as usual, he disappeared. And suddenly I heard steps behind me. Somebody was following me." Her face was tense. Kent could see that she was reliving that moment of fear which had probably haunted her all these past days. Drops of perspiration were forming on her upper lip. "I swung around and came face to face with him, a red-haired boy with a red beard. There aren't a lot of redheads around, and the ones I know don't have a beard. I used what I've learned in judo. I managed to throw him down and . . . and . . ."

she stammered, pulled herself together and went on. "But he got up, caught hold of me, and there I was on the ground, and he on top of me. He pulled out a knife..."

She could feel her father's hand closing around hers but paid no attention to it. "If Zero hadn't appeared suddenly and bitten him ... do you think the boy wanted to kill me?"

A red-haired boy in a dinky apartment in Philadelphia. Jacob Summerfield, who had vented his fury and hatred on him. Again Kent controlled his voice, spoke softly, trying to convince her that she had not been in danger of death. "Of course not. He just wanted to let you know that you should offer no resistance when he tried to rape you."

"But I didn't want to be raped."

"That's why he let you see the knife."

"Is that what you think?"

Kent nodded. Looking down at his daughter, he realized that Kate was no longer a little girl but a desirable creature. It was hard to grasp. Perhaps all fathers tended to see their daughters as eternally children. Still he said, "There must have been other boys who tried to make love to you."

"Of course." Kate pulled her hand away from his. "But we talked about it. I haven't had any sex with anyone yet, if you want to know. And that makes for a challenge. Sometimes I thought I should, with Jerry, so everybody'd know I was his girl and not dare to touch me. He's pretty strong and would protect me. But I really don't like him well enough to give in. He's so clumsy. Every time he sticks his hand into my blouse, I get green and blue spots."

The idea of fat little Jerry trying to make love to Kate was disgusting to Kent. "But this one was silent," Kate went on. "No arguments. And that's what I think frightened me most. Why do boys or men want to rape?"

"I guess it's a complex, a feeling that they're unable to get what they want otherwise, a lack of communication. Or maybe it gives them a feeling of superiority to rely on force."

"Crazy," said Kate. "Sick." She paused. "Thomas, maybe I should have given in to him. I mean, if I had, Zero would still be alive."

134

"Thank God you didn't," Kent answered. "It may sound hard, but you have to stop brooding about things that can't be changed."

Kate was silent for a moment, then she said, "I'll try. But promise me something, Thomas — don't tell Mom."

Strange how both of them were always trying to protect Kitty from anything that might upset her, Kitty, who seemed so strong. But was she? Kent had never wondered before if perhaps it was just a pose. "I have to tell her about Zero," he said.

Kate nodded. "But not about the boy."

Kent thought it over for a while, then he said, "I promise."

"Good," said Kate. "Because for me it all hangs together — the letter, the attack on me, Zero being poisoned . . ."

Of course she was right. "Very possibly," Kent answered, and then, repeating what he had said before, "but you must promise me not to brood about anything which can't be changed. Try to go back to sleep now; try to think of your birthday party and what fun it will be." He patted her shoulder and left the room, his knees shaking. He went into his study and called the police and the F.B.I. and repeated what Kate had just revealed to him. To his horror he was told that the boy had been interviewed by them before the attack, made a harmless impression, was let go, and now they had lost all trace of him. Then he went to make some fresh tea for Kitty.

But Kate found it impossible to sleep. She could hear her mother's high excited voice. "Zero poisoned. Bill Ward strangled. Kent, we've got to take Kate away. Please. I beg you. I can't stand this tension any longer. Every breathing moment of my life I feel something is going to happen to Kate."

Kate dragged herself out of bed and went into her mother's room. "Cool it, Mom," she said. "Don't get hysterical. It won't bring Zero back. I'm sure neither of us wants Thomas to kill himself to relieve your . . . well, your fear for my safety. Please love him a little more than me. Of course I'll go anywhere you want me to go. I could miss school. There are only a few more days left

135

anyway. Why make such a fuss about Zero when you never cared for him?"

Kitty didn't deny it. "I've never cared for dogs," she said, "but I liked Zero, even though he shed a lot."

"If Zero shed, it was my fault," said Kate. "I should have groomed him better."

"That's not the point," Kitty said sharply. "You know very well why I'm so excited. Bill Ward murdered. Zero poisoned. It all has to do with the letter."

Kate followed her father into the kitchen. "Don't be upset, Thomas," she told him. "She doesn't really love me more than you." And, oh, how that letter has changed us all she thought. Thomas drinks too much and Mom's started to smoke, and I'm afraid for the first time in my life. But Thomas is right. I mustn't brood about things that can't be changed. Just as Thomas has got over the crashing of his plane, I must get over the shock of Zero's death. If that letter hadn't come, he wouldn't be nervous, Mom wouldn't be either. I can grieve for Zero, but... She pulled herself together.

"Do you want your eggs? We've got some Canadian bacon. Or can I make you a mushroom omelet?"

"Just plain scrambled eggs," said Kent. "On the wet side if you can manage it."

As she put the platter before him, he caught her hand and held it to his cheek, his eyes resting on her, full of admiration. Kate forced herself to smile.

During his lunch hour, Sam Slew drove in. He got out of his car and before saying hello to either Kitty or Kent, he handed Kate a tiny dog. A puppy. A toy poodle.

"I don't want another dog," Kate told him rudely.

"If you don't accept one now," said Sam, "you never will."

"I don't like toy dogs. Think of humans bred to the size of dolls. Atrocious." But the poodle had round, shiny, black-button eyes and wagged his stubby little tail, nipped off at just the right length.

"Paper trained," said Sam. "It'll take three more months before she's housebroken. She's two months and three weeks old. And poodles are nice dogs." To Kitty,

"And they don't shed. Did you know that they were used once in France for hunting?"

"I'll keep her," said Kate, "until you find another home for her. And you'd better be quick about it. What's her name?"

"A long one," said Sam, "French. But it's on the pedigree." He handed her a piece of paper from the American Kennel Club. "Ninon de Lenclos," read Kate. "Who was she?"

"I think she was a courtesan," said Sam. "Look her up in the Britannica."

An hour later Anna came by. She was driving, had been driving now for over a week. She reached back into the car as she was getting out and emerged with a puppy, a young mastiff. "Jerry came by and told me...His name is Florian. He'll grow up to be a powerful dog. I hope you like him."

"I feel like the proprietor of a kennel," said Kate. "But thank you anyhow. If I give him back to you, I hope you won't mind. You could do with a dog yourself."

"I'll take him back any time you want me to," said Anna. "I'm sorry about Zero."

"I know you are."

"Where is your mother?"

"Right now she's at the hairdresser's, this being Tuesday. Thomas told her to go right ahead with the plans she'd made for today, so she's going to New York to see the play they got tickets for weeks ago. But Thomas didn't feel like going."

"Where's your father?"

"Up in his cage, telephoning. You're in love with him, aren't you?" She asked, not really asking but more to empty her mind which seemed like a squirrel in a cage treading the wheel, spinning around Zero and her red-headed attacker.

"I don't know who isn't." Anna laughed.

"Jerry's mother..." said Kate, "she's got a mirror in her window, a spyglass I think they call it, and she told her husband the other day...well, Jerry didn't get it all but from what he told me...you kissed."

"Maybe we did. Just as I'd kiss a big brother, if I had

137

one." Anna took Kate's hand and pressed it. "But do tell Thomas I'm here. If he doesn't want to come down, it's all right. But if he does, disappear, will you? And take care of Florian until you've made up your mind whether you want to keep him or not. Remember, you don't have to."

Kate went upstairs. "Thomas, Anna is here. She's brought me a dog too, a mastiff. She wants you to come down. I'll be busy getting the poodle and the mastiff acquainted, so please don't want me for anything."

Kent went downstairs. Kate had disappeared. "I haven't seen much of you lately. I'm sorry I was so busy."

He was, thought Anna, unusually pale. "I understand. And now Zero's death. Jerry told me. I just brought Kate a puppy. She's in the garage with him. But of course he's no replacement for Zero. He was as good as a body-guard for Kate. You and Kitty must be terribly upset."

"If it hadn't been for Zero," Kent sat down on the stoop in front of the kitchen door. "If it hadn't been for Zero . . ." he repeated. Anna waited patiently until he began to speak again. "She was attacked."

"When? By whom?"

"Remember the red-headed boy I wanted to see at Gordon's? Jacob Summerfield, the oldest son of the man I saw in Philadelphia, who was blinded? He blamed me for the crash. I've suspected him ever since I went there. And the description Kate gave me fits him. Maybe he just wanted to rape her, but he had a knife. Ever since she told me I've been phoning the police, the F.B.I. I hope to God they'll find him."

Anna's voice sounded as if she was fighting back tears. "Poor Kate. What a terrible shock it must have been for her. And for Kitty."

"Kitty doesn't know," Kent told her. "Kate and I agreed not to add to her fears. And Kate's right. I'm sure he's no longer in the neighborhood. Zero almost bit him to pieces, but we've got to find him."

"At least you've got a suspect now. Anything I can do for you?"

"Nothing at the moment."

"I'll phone you later."

25

From Kent's house Anna drove straight to Mario's beauty parlor, known to be the best in town, and spotted Kitty's car in the lot reserved for his customers. She parked hers close to it. Although Kate had said Kent had told Kitty to go ahead with whatever plans she had made for the day, after what Kent had told her, Anna felt a strong urge to keep Kitty at home.

After a while, she saw Kitty emerging from the back door, and honked sharply to get her attention. Kitty came over at once, her face smooth, her pumpkin colored hair set in a different way that made her look younger. Nobody would have guessed what she had been through all these weeks.

"It's good to see you driving again," she said.

"It's a great feeling," Anna smiled, "a new kind of freedom. Kate told me where you were. I thought it would be nice if we could all spend some time together."

"Sorry," said Kitty, "but I'm going to New York, and I'm late already." She gave herself a little shake. "Too unnerved to stay round here." She threw back her head. "I may not show it; I try not to, but I don't know how good I am at hiding my feelings. First it was Bill Ward's death. That upset me terribly, although everybody tries to assure me it needn't have had any connection with the job we gave him to do. But Zero's death has thrown me completely. As long as Zero was there I always felt he'd let no harm come to Kate. Why was he poisoned? To rob Kate of whatever protection he could give her. Obviously."

"Kent feels the same way."

"How do you know?"

Anna, alerted by the sudden animosity in Kitty's voice,

said as calmly as she could, "I've just come from your house. I brought Kate a puppy, a mastiff. He'll make a good watchdog."

"Was that the reason? Or did you want to see Kent?"

Anna opened the door of the car. "Please get in. Give me a little time."

"You're the last person I want to be with today."

"Why?"

"Anna, you know very well why. There's talk about you and Kent."

What made Anna seem on the one hand so primitive, on the other so fascinating, was her absolute inability to lie. "I'm sorry," she said. "You've heard some gossip, but it's not true, Kitty. Perhaps Kent and I are more intimate, but you have nothing to worry about."

"If you think your honesty touches me, you're wrong. You're honest because you feel guilty."

Anna pulled out a pack of cigarettes, offered Kitty one, lighted it for her, then took one herself. "You didn't let me finish," she said. "Please hear me out. I love him, but he loves you, needs you." She almost added, "And right now, when he's just found out about Kate having been attacked, you leave him alone." But knowing that Kent and Kate had decided not to upset Kitty by telling her, she remained silent.

"How very kind of you to tell me that," said Kitty.

Anna went on as if she hadn't heard Kitty's snide remark. "He needs distraction."

"So do I."

Again Anna ignored Kitty's remark. "When you two are together, I think you are unable to bury the tension that fills you both. It stands like a wall between you; against which both of you beat your heads in vain."

"I'm sure there are other women with whom he could find relaxation."

Anna spoke carefully. "I doubt it. You see, he's got to be able to talk about his worries, and the way he is, he would never mention them to a stranger. And he can't talk freely about them to you, not without adding to your worries. But with me ... I'm not his wife, and I'm not

140

Kate's mother, and that's why I'm the right company for him. But that's all." And I was always right for him, she thought. "He's so tense," she went on, "so pitifully tense."

"You think I don't know it?" Kitty had to make a tremendous effort to keep her voice from rising. "The other day he bought a pistol. And now he's teaching Kate and me how to shoot. He's put up a target behind the garage. Why in the world do you assume I'm not just as tense as he is?"

"I just tried to explain why your being together has to be a failure," Anna wanted to say, but caught herself at the last moment. "Because he's more emotional than you."

"I'm emotional all right," Kitty cried angrily. "If you think I don't care more for Kate than for my own life, you're wrong."

"And what about Kent?"

"He's part of my life, that goes without saying. Both of you are just using that letter as an excuse."

Are we? Anna asked herself. Is that why Kent finally showed tenderness, desire for me? Is that letter, with the fear it instills in all of us, the reason we are behaving so irrationally? And what is it doing to Kate? Is she really not scared, or is she pretending? Are none of us strong enough to cope with tragedy or to face terror? Are none of us noble enough to struggle through a perhaps hopeless situation without becoming greedy, without wanting to take advantage of a chance to fulfill desires that until now were controlled by decency? "Anyway," she said, "that's all I wanted to tell you."

"What *did* you want to tell me? Really?"

"Not to waste a thought on Kent and me."

26

THIS TIME KITTY went straight to Forster's apartment. Max had been waiting tea for her. There was a three-tiered, English mahogany stand with thin, sliced brown bread, scones and jelly, and a large chocolate cake decorated with the first new cherries. The sight of all the food made Kitty feel slightly sick.

"I can't eat a thing."

"But you will," said Maximilian. A moment later his man servant came in with iced champagne and a small tray arranged like a chessboard, with pieces of toast spread with red and black caviar. He put one small piece into her mouth and she almost closed her teeth on his fingers. He smiled, but he didn't tell her that she looked beautiful or prettier than ever. Instead he shook his head. "You're pale and you seem harassed."

"I am."

"Is that why you came?"

"I suppose so."

She took out her new powdercase and lipstick. She had done so several times while driving into town, but it hadn't stayed on. She licked her lips and some of the rouge away with it. She couldn't understand why it suddenly seemed to her so utterly disgusting to imagine Kent and Anna in bed together. Because Anna was crippled?

"Bill Ward is dead," she said.

"Who is Bill Ward?"

"Don't you remember? I told you about him. The detective we engaged to track down who wrote the letter."

"Didn't I tell you that was as good as impossible?"

"He was found murdered, strangled in some car."

Maximilian stirred his champagne to get the fizz out. "I think I read about it in the paper. But I don't see why

142

you're so worried about Ward's death. A man like that . . .
they always run the risk of being knocked off."

"But Kent and I think he may have found the person
who wrote the letter."

He took her in his arms.

When Kitty entered his bedroom, he was already in
bed, reading. The exhilarating scent of French soap and
bathoil filled the room. The curtains were drawn against
the daylight, and the air conditioning was turned on.
"Your tub is waiting for you," he said, without taking his
eyes off the paper. But when she came back, after having
taken her time to soak, he looked up. She was wearing
one of his silk robes. "Throw it off," he said, "if you want
to give me pleasure. I'd like to see you walk toward me
naked. You have such a beautiful proud walk, and last
time you were so shy."

I've been told that before, thought Kitty, and
straightened up.

"This is better," he said after a while. "Isn't it? Much
better than last time."

And so it was. And it came as an enormous surprise to
her that she was apparently a much more sensuous woman
than she had believed. Suddenly she saw herself in a
quite different light. Or did all people under stress resort
to sex as the most satisfactory distraction? She couldn't
help thinking of what Anna had said, and had to admit
to herself, however reluctantly, that right now, what Max
had to offer was somehow fitting. Perhaps this should
make her see Kent's turning to Anna for the same consolation in a different light?

She thought of the men and women she had known
who had had to face great difficulties, even tragedies, and
how they had reacted. Some had started to drink heavily,
others had tried to kill their fear by over-eating. Well,
she had started to drink, to smoke, but nothing had been
as satisfying as this . . . this going to bed with a man who
was not her husband. It gave her a respite from fear, it
relaxed her. But to sleep with a man she didn't love was
something she had never thought she would be able to do.
Men did, as Kent had told her, without getting involved,

and suddenly she could understand it. Not that she wanted to understand it. And being with Max had nothing to do with her feelings for Kent. Or had it?

It would have been wonderful if she could have forgotten Kent. "Wonderful and all wrong," she answered, choosing her words carefully. "I'm the wife of another man whom I think I love and the mother of his daughter. And here I am with you. Does that mean I just had to escape into this, or that I no longer love Kent?"

Max sat up in bed and lighted a cigarette. "Oh, dear." He shook his head. "Don't you know yet that in marriage, sex becomes a habit? And often loses its fascination? You know each other too well, and that's a bore. And because it's a bore, marriages break up, whatever other fine excuses the man and woman in question may think up. Everyone wants something new after a while, something different. Why should sex be an exception? And unfortunately, this is what two people who love and respect each other can't always produce, to be different. Some marriages of course last, but these are mostly without sex, and both parties have agreed that friendship suffices, or for reasons of tradition, has to suffice."

"Well, isn't friendship the most important, the lasting thing?"

"For some people. But one can still be friends and have affairs."

"I'm not so sure."

Max laughed. "Then why did you come back? Not that you slept with me the first time because you wanted to. You were so frightened, you could just as well have thrown yourself from the Empire State Building. But today? Today you're very different. You're responding more. I'll tell you something you'll deny. You have always wanted to sleep with me."

Kitty denied it.

"Oh, come on. Be honest. You were a kid then, a proud little kid whom I had offended. And you were still a virgin."

Kitty nodded.

"But you aren't a virgin any longer. A young virgin is

144

bad enough because they usually smell, but an old virgin is ghastly. And sleeping with only one man, how long is it? Sixteen years or more, it seems absolutely atrocious to me."

"Give me a cigarette," said Kitty. "Kent sleeps with other women."

"Most men do, and every grown woman takes it for granted and doesn't ask questions. Grow up, Kitty."

"I am growing up. Rapidly."

"I hope so."

"And in a little while you'll know me inside out and it will be finished."

"Very probable. But why not enjoy it while it lasts?"

"In other words, what you're trying to tell me is that after you I'll go to bed with another man."

"I imagine you will. But you'll always have your husband to fall back on."

Suddenly Kitty was in tears. They were streaming down her cheeks. Max put out his hand to wipe them away, tasted his finger. "Salty," he said, smiling.

"Oh, Max, do be serious for a moment. Don't you realize what a miserable situation I'm in? There's Kent, to whom I belong, or who belongs to me, and there's Kate, who means the world to me. And there's the letter demanding Kent's death if Kate is to live."

"And there you are, possibly having to make a choice between them."

She clutched his arm. "Don't say that. It's bad enough as it is. Our dog has been poisoned. He always guarded Kate, and Kent . . ."

She was totally under the influence of terror, and Maximilian thought of the terror that had gone on throughout history. It was why the Nazis had been so successful in cowering the Germans, because they had succeeded in spreading terror through every home. The whites in Africa, the communists in Russia . . . and the terror he was able to arouse.

"And Kent? How does he feel about it?"

"Kent is terrified too. He's teaching Kate and me how to shoot."

"Very wise of him."

Maximilian got up to fetch another bottle of champagne and two glasses. He tasted the first, then gave her one. "I don't know your husband," he said, "so I can't judge. Do you know if he loves his life more than he loves Kate?"

"What do you mean?"

"I'm asking you — is he the kind of man who would kill himself to save his daughter?"

"I don't know," said Kitty. "I don't think so. No, I don't know. I'm afraid of every possibility. That he might sacrifice his life, although he loves life so much. That Kate could be hurt, or killed. And I love them both."

"And he might have to make that choice."

"If one could only know, could find out if it's just a crank's letter or a serious threat one could perhaps do something — anything. But as it is we fluctuate from one hour to the next. If it's meant Kent says that man will find Kate wherever we might hide her. If it's just a crank we should not pay any attention to it. But Zero has been poisoned ... What am I to do before I go insane?"

27

"WOULD YOU HAVE a pizza with Kate and me?" Kent asked Anna over the phone. "We're ready to go any time. We'll pick you up."

"Can you give me half an hour?"

"We'll be there in thirty minutes sharp."

Anna laughed. "I didn't mean it that precisely. You can be late. I'll wait for you."

They were lucky; they got a booth. Kent liked the place because there weren't any juke boxes in the booths, only one huge one, with lurid green and orange lights in the back of the restaurant, next to some pinball machines. Every few minutes Kate disappeared to put in a quarter for some of her favorite records. When she was not at the table, Anna said, "Thomas, I saw Kitty before she drove into town. I'm afraid she's upset about us. She thinks we're having an affair. She was quite hostile to me. I tried to assure her that it was just our friendship that had deepened. We needed to help each other over what was happening."

"I had a long talk with Kitty the other night," said Kent. "Things are changing between us."

Anna thought of Gordon. She hadn't accepted his proposal of marriage yet. Perhaps she could postpone it a little longer, although Gordon was getting more and more impatient every day.

"I'd like to know what's on your mind," said Kent.

"All of it," said Anna. "The whole damn situation. And you and me."

Kate came back to the table. "Anna, would you mind terribly if I didn't keep the mastiff? He's a cute puppy, but I . . ."

"I understand," said Anna, "but I don't think I

can take care of him as he has to be cared for right now."

"Don't worry. I talked to Jerry. He's going to house-break him, and maybe then you'd like to have him. Jerry says mastiffs are good watchdogs. He says he'll probably grow to weigh a hundred and seventy pounds when he's full grown. I'm not going to keep the poodle Sam brought me either. I can't understand why people are so dumb as to think I'd want another dog after Zero."

"Well, what kind of an animal would you like?"

"When I was a child, I wanted a panda, now I think I'd prefer a lion cub."

"But you wouldn't be able to keep it," said Kent, "and I'm no gamewarden who could furnish the facilities. We'd have to move to Africa."

"Why not?" said Kate. "Wouldn't be such a bad way of getting away from here."

Kent and Anna looked at each other. "Even then," said Kent, "you'd have to set the lion free one day, just as your beloved Elsa had in the end to be taught to shift for herself."

"Why is it that one always has to lose what one loves best?" asked Kate, munching on a piece of pizza that had meanwhile grown cold.

"Because that's life," said Kent. "With its two sides. One is happiness, the other unhappiness. You see, you can only be really unhappy about something that has been really happy."

"You sound like Mr. Hulbert," said Kate, then corrected herself. "I shouldn't have said that. He was terribly nice to come and read my favorite psalm over Zero." She closed her eyes and recited, "Yea, though I walk in the shadow of the valley of death, I shall fear no evil. You know, it did something for me. I guess I was silly to say what I did, about getting away from here. But things *are* beginning to get me down." She looked at her father. "Maybe it's catching. Sometimes Mom stares at me as if I were dead already and she was viewing a corpse. You don't stare at me, Thomas. You only stare at your gun. I wish you'd throw it away."

"But you've become quite a good shot," said Kent. "Don't you think it's fun?"

"It might be, if it wouldn't remind me of that letter. Every time you take that gun in your hand, I'm thinking . . ."

How Zero's death, and the inevitable connection it brought with it between the boy who had assaulted her had changed the child's outlook. Or had it just brought fear to the surface, which would be a mixed blessing.

"When I see you eye the target, I get the feeling that you've had it. That you love me so much, you'd be willing to bow out for my sake. And I'm terrified that you'll make the wrong decision. For where would I be if I lost you too? Without you, without Zero . . ."

"Don't you love your mother?" asked Anna softly.

Kate frowned. "I do. But I think I love Thomas more. I think Mom and I are too much alike. I know you'll tell me it's just that I'm at the age when I resent authority, but that's not it. I just love them in different ways. I loved Zero, but that was different too. I love Jerry, even though he can make me furious. Thomas, please throw your gun away. It frightens me more than anything else. Yes, more than anything else."

"I promise you not to kill myself," said Kent, his voice serious.

"But will you keep your promise?"

"I'll keep my promise," said Kent, and held out his hand.

Kate took it and shook it. Then she went off to play the juke box again. From there they could see her wander off to a pinball machine that wasn't being used. Anna lighted a cigarette. "Thomas, do you realize what you've just done? By promising Kate not to kill yourself, you've made her think she'll be sacrificed so you can live. Probably that's what she wants, still she's going to be in deadly fear that from now on, at any moment, something dreadful is going to happen to her."

Kent stared at her. She was right. "But my God, what am I to do? I know she loves me, depends on me. I've got to reassure her somehow. I can't tell her that I might have to make the choice."

Anna looked at him, her eyes filled with compassion. What an incredible dilemma to be in. Kate came back to them. "I want to go home," she said.

"So do I," said Anna. "I think all of us are ready for an early night."

"And you're not cross with me for giving your present to Jerry?"

"I'm never cross."

"I know," said Kate. "That's why you're such a comfort."

28

IT'S STRANGE HOW easily a man can change his mind. I always thought that I was one of those people who just had one idea at a time, one purpose, and would follow it through when the time was ripe. Well, I haven't changed my mind about accomplishing what I set out to do, just about the timing. Kent hasn't gone back to flying yet. He asked and was granted another four weeks of leave of absence. I guess he feels he's got to stick around to watch over Kate. He doesn't seem to be contemplating suicide, yet. But I'll get him to that point. I'm sure of that. Who was it that said, "He that can have patience can have what he will." Franklin, if I remember correctly. And Cervantes advised, "Patience, and shuffle the cards." Oh, I've been reading a lot lately. More than usual. Well, Kent is shuffling the cards too.

Why am I so pessimistic tonight? If pessimism is a religious disease, as some say, I'd be a religious man. Which I am not. Or am I? Perhaps in the sense that there are some things I try to believe in and wish I could be sure of, and therefore try to make them come to pass. Nobody will ever find out who wrote the letter unless my impatience becomes stronger than my reason and I commit an act of stupidity. And to me, stupidity is a sin. But I went to a lawyer in New York, a shyster. I put the case to him as if I were Kent. What would happen to a man who wrote the kind of letter I wrote? He had to look it up! Then he told me he thought it might be this or that, he'd have to study it further. Out for a good fee. Well, this and that are : Penalties for blackmail and attempted murder : An examination of the extortion sections of the New York Penal Code, numbers 115.05, 155.30 and 155.40, indicates that these sections are applicable to the situation in which a person makes the following threat : "If you don't commit suicide, I will murder your wife." There might also be a violation of code number 240.30 which is aggravated harassment. This section provides : "A person is guilty of aggravated harassment when, with intent to harass, annoy, threaten or alarm another person, he : (1) Communicates or causes a communication to be initiated by mechanical or electronic means or otherwise, with a person, anonymously or otherwise, by telephone or by telegraph, mail or any other form of written communication, in a manner likely to cause annoyance or alarm; or (2) Makes a telephone call, whether or not a conversation ensues, with no purpose of legitimate communication."

"Aggravated harassment is a misdemeanor and under code number 70.15 (1) the sentence shall be fixed by the court and shall not exceed one year.

The hypothetical fact pattern would also constitute a violation of code number 120.30 of the Penal Law which is promoting a suicide attempt. This section provides : "A person is guilty of promoting a suicide attempt when he intentionally causes or aids another person to attempt suicide."

Promoting a suicide attempt is a class E felony and under code number 70.00 the term shall be fixed by the court and shall not exceed four years.

It should be noted that there is a special section of the Penal Law 120.30, which defines when promoting a suicide attempt shall be punishable as an attempt to commit murder. This section provides : "A person who engages in conduct constituting both the offense of promoting a suicide attempt and the offense of attempt to commit murder may not be convicted of attempt to murder unless he causes or aids the suicide attempt by use of duress or deception."

Well, I know where I stand. Actually, I always have. I can read law just as well as any lawyer. Once you get used to their intricate ways of expressing themselves, it's easy. But what a fool I am to bother about all this. They've got a suspect now. Jacob Summerfield. Personally, I'd like to kill him for attacking Kate. But even if the F.B.I. finds him, it won't help Kent. He remains my victim.

What surprised me is that just a few weeks ago I was

quite satisfied with the changes going on between Kent and his wife, even in Kate, although it was never my intention to frighten her. But Kitty? This man Forster. She was seen entering his apartment. Twice. Kitty Kent. Ice on the inside and a book of morals on the surface. But if you could rouse her . . . but that's another story.

Why am I no longer content with the terror I have instilled? I mean, where do you draw the line between hate and love? Both are strong passions, fundamental, like hunger and thirst. A man who can't love, can't hate, and vice versa. And hate can turn into love just as love can turn into hate at the drop of a hat, just like in a poker game, when one card can make all the difference. You either draw an ace, or a royal flush, or a full house. I don't care for all these new varieties of poker. For me it's an old-fashioned game, draw poker, five cards and you discard what you think doesn't have a chance, and buy in.

Is it in my nature that I can't be patient? I, who have tried to make a virtue of patience, kowtowing to people I thoroughly dislike, biding my time until I could get them to help me. I, who have slaved to get where I am today. A rich man. A much richer man than anyone suspects. With quite a bit of money stashed away in Switzerland. I still believe in a nation that manages not to be caught up in war and gets along with almost every other country. Maybe because of their bank secrecy? God knows, with the way the economy is going . . . will they stand up if the gold standard is abandoned? May be. I do everything correctly, officially. No secret accounts for me. Except a very small one nobody will be able to trace.

But why am I so impatient? If I'd set myself a time limit for Kent to kill himself, I could understand it. Then I'd have to live up to a certain date. So far I haven't done that. I guess I wanted them to live in uncertainty and fear more than I actually wanted to carry out my threat. Sometimes I even feel sorry I sent the letter. Yet I know damn well I'll send another. Why? And how will Kent react to it? Two interesting questions. They say curiosity is the sign of an alert intelligence. According to that I should be more intelligent than I give myself credit for.

29

Iᴛ ᴡᴀs Kɪᴛᴛʏ who went to get the mail. Kent was in the city, keeping an appointment with the line office. A few more weeks and he'd be back on his job. Kitty didn't know whether to be glad or more distraught than she was already.

A blue paper envelope, the address printed in large, red block letters. She saw it at once between the others — bills, junk mail — and she stood as if paralyzed, as if she had reached out to touch a poisonous snake. Later she never remembered how long it had actually taken for her to touch it, and then she carried it, separate from all the other mail, all by itself in her left hand, as if her left hand didn't count for much. When she got back to the house she dropped it in Kent's cage, on the long table, and slammed the door hard, as if she could slam reality away.

She made the beds, she cleaned the tub, she dusted, she watered the garden, she brewed herself a cup of coffee in the Melita cup, folding the paper carefully before she ladled out the spoons of coffee and poured boiling water over them. She made several routine calls, to order meat, to cancel her cleaning lady and appointment to play bridge at three. Then she thought of her mother's advice. "If you expect bad news, fill your stomach first." She scrambled two eggs, cut some ham meticulously into tiny pieces. Her heart would not stop pounding. Then she went upstairs and looked at the letter. It wasn't addressed to her, but, again, to Kent. Mailed in New York. GPO. She took it into her bedroom with her and lay down on the bed, putting the letter, unopened, on the second pillow. She lay there beside it, awake, her eyes wide open. Now and then she looked at it and it seemed to coil into a little blue snake with a fiery red head. She screamed and threw her pillow over it. But it seemed to crawl out from under the pillow, a piece of blue paper now, but alive.

She tore it open. It read, "If within fourteen days from now you haven't killed yourself, your daughter Kate will die." She looked at the date on the envelope, counted on her fingers — that would be July 13th. She read it again. It didn't come out right. She counted again. And again was wrong. She reached for her calendar on the night table. This and that, unimportant things. Only one day was marked in red. July 11th. Kate's fifteenth birthday. Scribbled underneath it: big party. Have it catered. Engaged band. Cross out with "done." July 13th would be a Sunday.

July thirteenth.

She knew she should call the F.B.I., but couldn't make herself get up to go into Kent's study to phone from there or unplug the phone and bring it to her bedroom. She let the calendar slip to the floor and lay on her bed as if paralyzed. She couldn't even remember where Kent was, and it took a great deal of mental effort to recall where he had gone and that he'd said he'd be back in the early afternoon. Usually he kept his word. She buried her face in the pillow. If he came home as promised, he would be here in a short while. No use to try to reach him there. He'd already be on his way. Besides, she couldn't make herself move. So she lay motionless. She couldn't even answer his call when he entered the house. Her voice seemed to have been blotted out by sheer terror.

"Not feeling well?" Kent asked when he came into her bedroom and found her lying on the bed. And coming closer, "You look like a ghost and you're trembling all over. What's wrong?"

Kitty could only move her head sideways. He saw the blue envelope marked with red block letters. He swallowed once or twice before he picked it up, read it, made for the door. Suddenly Kitty could speak again. "Don't leave me. Where are you going? Where's Kate?" Odd that in all this time she hadn't thought of her daughter.

"Kate is at Anna's," he said. "And I'm going to call the

F.B.I. I'll be right back. Or have you called them already?"

Kitty shook her head.

It seemed a long time until he came back to sit at her bedside. "They want this new piece of evidence as soon as possible."

"Don't leave me alone. Not yet. You can go in later, but not right now."

Kent got up, went to the bathroom and came back with a glass of water and a yellow pill. "Here, take this. It will help you to calm down. You used to give it to me when I had nightmares."

Obediently, like a child, she swallowed the valium. "It's an ultimatum, isn't it?"

"That's the way it's phrased. But a crank's ultimatum mightn't mean anything. Just some kind of satisfaction, like holding someone else's fate in his hand. Self-indulgence in the power he imagines he exercises."

"Is that what the F.B.I. said?"

Kent nodded.

"I don't believe they're going to be of much use. According to the papers, so many cases remain unresolved."

And they haven't found Jacob Summerfield, yet, thought Kent.

"What are we to do?" asked Kitty. "Kent, what are we to do? And you and I are no longer the same. Everything is wrong between us. We can't even talk as we used to do. If we do at all, it always revolves around this problem, and if it doesn't, we both try to think up something which has nothing to do with it at all." She shuddered as she thought of their agonized attempts to find subjects away from their terror. They no longer exchanged views on economic or political events, on their home, Kate, their plans for the future. It no longer occurred to them to point to the humming bird sucking at a delphinium blossom, or to be distracted by the beauty of a flowering tree or that suddenly moles were marring their lawn, the boring daily events that needed attention, like the pool filter not working right, or a door that had warped, always trying to get away from discussing mental and physical cruelty as if they had never heard of people afflicted by them, and never seeing eye to eye when they couldn't help mentioning them. Kent saw them as a sickness, for Kitty they were a way of life for some people. But to Max she could talk endlessly about it. He listened with the patience and understanding of an outsider and could usually calm her. Doubtlessly Anna served similarly as a sounding board for Kent.

"And in the meantime Anna and you and I and..."

"Don't give it a thought," he said. "Whatever has happened is unimportant."

"Is it?"

"To me it is."

Kitty, unused to tranquilizers, began to feel the effect of the valium. I was a fool, she thought, not to have taken it before. "But what are we to do, Kent?"

"I asked for a guard for Kate. She's got to be put under surveillance."

"And they're going to send someone?"

"Yes. A Miss Brown."

"And if she doesn't work out?"

"She will. Don't be so pessimistic."

"I can't help it. I'm so afraid that this maniac might kill you, not Kate. I can't imagine anyone shooting a little girl, when what he wants is for you to commit suicide. I keep thinking he added this threat only to make it more imperative that you kill yourself."

"That's possible," Kent said. "It came to my mind too. But you must stop thinking along these lines. If something like that happens, it would be fate."

"But I don't believe in predestination. I think we are masters of our fate."

"So do I. And that's why I've made up my mind to take you and Kate away for a while. When I drive in now to deliver the letter, I'll pick up three tickets for us. The day after the party we're leaving for England. You and Kate will stay there while I'll try to be put on another flight route, say London-Rome, or Paris-Rome... wherever they have a spot for me during the next few months. You'd better get ready for a long absence from here."

157

Kitty sighed. "It does offer a chance. Oh, Kent, I do love you."

"I know," he said, "and you know that there isn't another woman I'd want to share my life with."

"But..."

"No buts," he said. "How terror made us behave will no longer be important once it's all over."

"I wish you'd tell me when that will be."

"I wish I could. In the meantime let's try and stick it out together." Then, unexpectedly they heard Sam Slew's voice. "Anybody home?"

"Come up," yelled Kent. "We're both taking a rest."

Sam stuck his head in at the bedroom door. "I didn't mean to intrude," he said, "but somebody pinched one of my pistols, or I must have left it here, the Colt I tried out on your target. I just wondered..."

His eyes fell on the letter Kent had brought back from his study. "Another one of those. Allow me." He picked it up, read it, put it down and shook his head. He looked at them, his expression horror-stricken.

They stared at each other in desperation. "If that bastard means what he said, I can only think of a ruse," Sam said finally.

"What kind of a ruse?" Kitty and Kent asked simultaneously.

"I'm sure the police and whatever other authorities might be involved would cooperate. And certainly your doctor would."

"In what?"

"Have Kent officially commit suicide, so that the crank is convinced he killed himself. The coffin wouldn't have to be open. Someone who shoots himself through the mouth is not a pretty sight. The minister could hold a wonderful sermon, everybody who'd ever known Kent would show up. You would be cremated, Kent. At least you told me once that was what you wanted. Of course you would have to disappear a day or two before, and after the funeral...well, you'd have to stay away for a while. Europe possibly. And after a few months, Kitty and Kate could follow you."

"I read something like that, or saw it on television. A man had to disappear and he did just that to mislead people who were after him."

"Everything's been done," said Sam. "So what's wrong with it?"

"And what about Kate?" asked Kitty, suddenly taken with the idea.

"Of course one would have to tell her the truth." Sam smiled. "But I think she's a good enough little actress to play the part of the bereft daughter."

"I'd rather see her in another role," Kent frowned. "Besides, the trick mightn't work. That paranoiac might find out."

"Why don't you suggest it to the F.B.I.?" asked Kitty. "See what they think of it." Somehow Kent's earlier proposal to go away for God knew how long had upset her unreasonably. Alone in London, seeing Kent only at intervals. "At least we'd all gain some time during which they might find the maniac."

Instead of answering, Kent picked up the letter. "I'd better be on my way."

Kitty panicked again. "Not yet. Don't leave me yet. After all they know about it, what does an hour more or less matter?"

Sam stared at her. "Are you afraid something might happen to Kent?"

"I am," said Kitty, her voice barely audible.

"You're not going to commit suicide, are you, Kent?" Sam asked. "Just to save Kate?"

"Never," said Kent.

"But somebody might kill him." Kitty put both hands in front of her face to hide it.

"Then I'll take the letter into New York," said Sam. "Just let me have the address and the name of the guy to whom I'm to deliver it."

30

THE BODYGUARD KENT and Kitty engaged for Kate was introduced to her as a distant relative of her mother, a Miss Beatrice Brown. Kitty called her Cousin Bea, Kent called her Miss Bea, but to Kate she was Cousin Brown.

Kate was not sure if this was a lie but decided not to voice her doubt. If Thomas did not want her to know he liked another person around for protection, she would play along. She was a formidable lady, "As tall as she's square," Kate described her to Jerry, "and I'm sure she wears a wig. Maybe she's bald. She looks old enough to have lost her hair. And the way she dresses! Long skirts, and boots like you and me, and she's got a leather jacket I'd like to pinch, if it was my size."

"Maybe I could wear it," suggested Jerry, whose black leather jacket looked worn. "But why did she move in with you?"

Kate laughed. "Thomas said relatives are also people. I never thought of them that way. I thought they were family. Mom showed me a photograph in her old album where Miss Brown almost looks pretty. Anyway, I think she's a lesbian; was long before women were liberated. Just the way she hangs around me. But she doesn't say much, and she does play a formidable game of gin. Beat me twice, and in scrabble. Oh God, she knows more words than there are in the dictionary."

"What about chess?" asked Jerry. "I'll take her on. I bet she's better than you or Thomas."

"Funny creature." Kate shook her head. "She sits in her room like a bird on its nest, protecting its young. When I want to go out, she asks very politely, would I mind if she came along. She's a good driver too."

"Could she handle my motorbike?"

"I'm sure she could. She thinks you're handsome."

"Seems to have good taste." Jerry took out a pocket comb and ran it through his brown, wavy hair.

"I wish you'd cut it shorter," said Kate, eyeing him critically. "In Europe I understand long hair is out."

"It is in some parts of the States," said Jerry, who was proud of his curls that fell almost to the nape of his neck. "Do you really mind?"

"Yes, I do. So cut it."

"There's something wrong with you," said Jerry. "You always mistake politeness for a real offer."

"Your fault," said Kate. "If you don't mean it, why offer it? You're a phony, that's what you are."

"You're a phony too. You make up stories all the time that aren't true."

"Because you bore me. And I don't make up all that many stories."

"You told me a boy tried to rape you in the park."

"I said a boy ran after me and it seemed to me . . ."

"In the park? There are always people walking there."

"Well, right then there weren't. There wasn't anybody."

"You really think he wanted to rape you?"

"What else?"

"I'd like to rape you."

"I'd like to see you try. Anyway, with Cousin Brown around, you wouldn't have a chance."

"She'd probably rape me first. Old spinsters are known to like young boys."

"Could be," said Kate, "but that I'd like to watch."

To her surprise, Jerry flushed crimson.

'You're blushing."

"Because you've changed such a lot."

"In what way?"

"It's hard to say."

"You're stupid."

But he wasn't, thought Kate. She *had* changed. At first, when she had read the letter Thomas had dropped, she had thought nothing of it. A little while later, warned to watch out for herself, she had suddenly felt important, the centre of some sort of sinister attraction. Then again her mind had swung around and she had realized that she wasn't the important one — the one who was being threatened was Thomas, and an anxiety she had never felt before had gripped her. Thomas loved her, she knew that, and the threat the letter imposed became agonizing. Would he kill himself to save her?

Sleepless hours at night, when formerly she had slept like a log, hours during which she was saving Thomas from any foolish action, such as doing away with himself, others in which she was a heroine, defending him. Successfully too. And of course hours, inspired by her parents' attitude, when she told herself that among the millions living in the United States, there had to be thousands of cranks who found satisfaction, or a reason for living, in writing scare letters just like that. But she couldn't deny any longer that the red-headed boy in the park had frightened her, and that without Zero ... no, don't think of Zero, she told herself. He had a good life and he didn't suffer too long. But Christ, how she missed him. And it took great effort not to show it, and to cry only in bed when she was certain nobody could hear.

She had no inkling of the second letter which threatened Thomas with an ultimatum, yet she had a definite feeling that he was deeply distressed and hardly able to hide it. Several times now he had closed the door to his study when Kitty joined him there. Usually he kept the door open. It was quite obvious that they were keeping something from her.

"You never gave your birthday party," said Jerry, "and we were all looking forward to it."

"I know. But Mom and I decided on a dance instead. Next week. At Jose's in Great Neck. There'll be forty of us."

"I didn't get an invitation."

"Impossible. I mailed it myself. You're going to be my escort."

"Sure you didn't forget to mail it?"

"Sure," said Kate, although she wasn't at all sure. Lately she had forgotten quite a few things which once she had done automatically.

"Did you invite that Travers shit?"

"Eddie is not a shit, and I certainly did invite him. I like him."

"I'll tell you why you like him." Jerry was furious. "Because he's older than all of us other guys. He's got a car, while I have to wait for graduation to get one."

"He's an improvement on you in other ways too."

"Thanks."

"He plays a better game of tennis, and I play better when there's more of a challenge."

"So that's the kind of a girl you are."

"Always was. I adore challenge. Brings out the best in me."

"He isn't much to look at."

"I don't judge people by their looks."

"You're lying again. You always go for the good-looking ones."

"Maybe I did when I was younger, and thought it was important. And I like his jazz. It isn't just stupid kid stuff, or like grown-ups showing off."

"Goddam the mosquitoes!" Jerry slapped his neck furiously. "And let me tell you something else. You've become smug."

"And you're a bore."

"So are you."

Kate smiled at him, a smile Jerry always found irresistible. Contrary to other people, she closed her eyes when she smiled, her lips parting as if ready for kissing, a dreamy expression on her face. If she hadn't opened her eyes again, almost at once, Jerry would have pounced. But she did open her eyes, and now she was looking at him critically. "I want you to look your best," she said. "No jeans. Grey flannel trousers and your nice blue jacket and tie."

"Shit. We'll all be uncomfortable. What's the matter with you? Turning West Egg?"

It took Kate a moment or two to remember that in "The Great Gatsby" King's Point had been renamed West Egg. "No," she said. "But Thomas bought me a lovely dress. I want to wear it and it wouldn't go at all with sweaty jeans and smelly sweaters. And all the girls are going to turn up in their best."

"Hurrah for Nassau County. Why for Christ's sake did our parents have to move to such a neighborhood?"

"It suits me fine," said Kate. "It has some beautiful estates, but for the likes of us just as many nice houses, swimming pool or no swimming pool. Once in a while it's fun to do something different."

"And your parents will be there, and Cousin Brown?"

"Your parents are invited too."

"And Anna?"

"Of course. She's one of my best friends."

"And your father's too."

"And my mother's."

Jerry said nothing, he just looked at Kate. They'd been going together for almost three years, and although he knew his parents didn't approve of the Kents, he was determined to marry her just as soon as it was humanly possible.

A small distance away, at the swimming pool, Kitty, Kent and Miss Brown were drinking beer. "That dance Kate is looking forward to so much," Kitty told Miss Brown, "is going to take place exactly two days before the ultimatum. I wonder if we shouldn't cancel it."

Miss Brown pulled at a hair that was growing out of a wart on the left side of her mouth. Twice a month it grew to a certain length; if she tried to tweeze it in its infant stage, it broke off, which invariably infuriated her. Now she looked in the direction of the red beech under which Jerry and Kitty were lying on a blanket. "I wouldn't cancel," she said. "I don't believe in ultimatums. But if that maniac means it, my experience is that he'll act on schedule. Besides, I'll be there." She pointed to the large pocket on the right side of her jacket where Kitty and Kent knew she carried her pistol.

"Somehow," said Kent, "I feel very strongly that I should see that woman in New York before the dance."

"Helga Johnson? Why? The F.B.I. checked her out."

164

"And Martin Cramer in Newark. They are two people I haven't met personally so far."

"You don't seem to have much confidence in us." Miss Brown sounded a trifle annoyed. "The F.B.I. is tops, Mr. Kent. Spare yourself the trouble. You wouldn't find out half as much as my bureau, whatever your personal impression might be — and I'm not saying it would be wrong — just that it could be wrong, colored by personal sympathy for instance, or justifications, or your efforts to get into another person's mentality. Sympathy and justification can be leads, certainly, but out of a thousand cases, ninety per cent of them are wrong. Leave it to the people who are trained to be objective, to deal with facts, who have all the data in their files — they'll get the scent, like hunting dogs."

She started to pull at the hair on her wart again, and Kitty said, "I have a very good pair of tweezers upstairs, not one of those short ones, but the long ones that are so hard to find in the States, and if you do, they're fiendishly expensive. If you want to come with me . . ."

Miss Brown laughed uproariously. "I don't know," she said, "but you always manage to startle me. One minute you're hysterical and the next . . . okay, I'll come up with you. But first send Jerry away and Kate to bed. It's almost eleven."

"There's no school."

"Never mind. When I was fifteen I had to go to bed at nine-thirty. If I had been obedient I was allowed to read for half an hour, but then my father or mother came into my room and it was lights out."

"But you had a flashlight to read under the cover, didn't you, Miss Bea?"

"Sure. Didn't we all?"

"But times have changed. Nowadays youngsters stay up as long as they please."

"Be that as it may," said Miss Brown, "I want Jerry sent home." She got up from her lounge chair to follow Kitty into the house. Kent went over to the red beech. "Time to go home, Jerry."

"I don't have to be in before twelve-thirty."

"But I want Kate to go to bed."

Jerry got up reluctantly. "Anyhow, too many mosquitoes here. We've got less at our place."

"Good for you," said Kent. "Good night, Jerry."

He sat down on the blanket next to Kate. Kate used the spray, first on her father, then on herself.

"What's going to happen, Thomas?"

"Happen?"

"I mean all the plans we made. First you were trying to talk me into camp again, and when I said absolutely no, unless they made me a counsellor, you were going to take me and Mom to Martha's Vineyard. Then, after that damn letter came, it was going to be Europe, or a camp in Switzerland. I'd like to know."

"We'll decide after the dance."

"Okay. I just don't like to feel like a letter that isn't delivered because someone forgot to put a stamp on it."

Kent laughed.

"Do you still love me?"

"Why shouldn't I love you?"

"Because . . . it's hard to say. Because I'm causing you so much worry."

"Kate, I thought you were adult enough to understand that if the writer of the letter hadn't used you as a threat, he would have used your mother."

"I thought about that."

"Good."

"But I want you to promise me again that you won't do anything to yourself just because of me."

"I promised you that already." But he sensed that she needed assurance, and he lifted his hand. "I hereby swear . . ." and as he finished the sentence he knew that the ruse of his official death, which he had discussed with Kitty, with Sam, even with the local police, was out. He got up, folded the blanket, and put his arm around Kate's shoulder. "I'll tell you a secret," he said. "I love you too much to leave you."

31

THE SPAGHETTI AND meatballs, the cold ham and potato salad, the crackers and cheese (not very much appreciated) and the cakes and cookies were gone. So was the punch Kent had mixed, and the soft drinks, and the beer for the older boys. Kitty began to feel whoozy. She was sitting in the rear of the private room they had rented, with the few grown-ups, parents of the boys Kitty liked best and to whom she felt under an obligation, and she was watching, rather amused, how much their age group, particularly the women, were enjoying one bottle of champagne after the other. Most of the men were sticking to whiskey. At one point there had been a discussion over the Kents engaging a band, who were playing black pants and red jackets, when quite a few of the youngsters were as good as the pros, at least in the opinion of their parents. "But then," Kent had explained, "Kate says the boys who can play well are also the best dancers, and she didn't want to miss them on the floor."

"But an entertainer," said Mrs. Travers, the wife of a very successful surgeon who had moved to King's Point recently. "Our Eddie knows a thousand tricks better than this man you got from New York."

Kent couldn't very well reveal the fact that the man was from the F.B.I.

Sam Slew said "I know better ones than either he or your son. He had only two pigeons. I could do it with ten if I had them handy."

He pulled a twenty dollar bill out of his pocket. "Anybody missing one?" Mrs. Travers was. She stared at him as he handed it back to her with a flourish. "Well . . ."

"Just tell me whom you'd like to have at our table?"

"My son, of course. He's dancing with Kate, way back

over there, but I must tell you, all the telepathy in the world won't pry him loose from his favorite girl."

"Not going to try telepathy," said Sam. "No good at it."

He reached under his seat and produced a coiled rope. Mrs. Travers' eyebrows went up in surprise. "Do you always carry a lasso?"

"When I want to have some fun with it," said Sam, "like tonight." He got up, loosening the noose at his side, waited for an opening, then let it fly across the floor and caught Eddie and Kate around the waist. Gently he drew them through the astonished crowd to their table.

"Formidable!" Miss Brown applauded. She was wearing a long silk skirt with a lace jacket, from under which her breasts showed, still she looked like an old-fashioned spinster, and unattractive.

"How mean you are, Sam." Kate looked furious. "Just when I was dancing with Eddie. He's by far the best around."

Eddie seemed to think it was a huge joke, until Jerry rushed up and said, "Thank you, Mr. Slew. Now I can dance with Kate." He lifted the rope and danced off with her. "Not fair!" shouted Eddie.

"Eddie deserves a glass of champagne," said his mother, filling one for him. He tossed it down, held out his glass for a refill. This time Sam filled it for him.

"I don't like that boy," Kitty whispered to Kent.

Miss Brown was looking at her. Kitty's face was ashen, beads of perspiration showed above her finely shaped, sensuous mouth. "You're not feeling too good, are you?" said Miss Brown, and marched Kitty off to the ladies room. When she came back, she nudged Kent. "You'd better take her home. She vomited, then almost fainted. Something doesn't seem to have agreed with her. I myself am off fish, since the waters are so polluted. But then what can you eat with all the poisonous sprays they still allow, and the coloring they put into almost every food to make it look fresh and more tasty? Take her home."

"Now? Before the grabbag?"

Miss Brown glanced at her mannish wrist-watch. "It's

eleven-thirty," she said. "The grabbag will take place twenty minutes from now, and then there'll be a last dance, maybe two. At twelve-thirty it'll be all over."

"Cousin Bea . . ." Kitty pleaded.

"Cousin Bea is here to watch out. And our magician is on the alert too.' She turned to Kent. "Take your wife home. Give her a sedative. You have nothing to worry about."

Kent touched Kitty's hand. It was ice cold. He felt her forehead. Hot and feverish. Miss Brown, he thought, and the magician were better watchdogs than either he or Kitty. He ordered another bottle of champagne, got up, asked Kitty to dance and danced her to the entrance. "We're going home."

"I don't want to go home. I want to stay to the end. Besides, it's impolite."

"Never mind. Kate will be home in less than an hour. And you don't want to stay here, shaking hands and saying thank you for coming. You're going to bed right now."

Too weak to muster any opposition, Kitty allowed Kent to lead her outside. "Oh, the fresh air feels good." She breathed deeply. "It was awfully stuffy in there, in spite of the airconditioning. Give me a few minutes out here, Kent, and I can go back and be the polite hostess."

"I appreciate the fact that you're trying to control yourself," he told her, putting his arm around her trembling shoulders and steering her to where he had parked their car. "But you need rest now, and I think we can trust Miss Brown and the magician, whatever his name is."

"Bartlett," said Kitty. "A nice man. He came yesterday to introduce himself. He slept at the Inn. Have you forgotten? You reserved a room for him and his assistant."

Kent hadn't forgotten. Barlett had made a good impression on him — calm, efficient, just as Miss Brown had described him. He pushed Kitty gently into the car. "We still have two days to go," he said, "if that lunatic means what he says. And I don't believe it for a moment. Anyway, twenty-four hours from now we'll be on a plane to London. I picked up the tickets today, reduction and all for the three of us. So stop worrying."

"Kate wanted the party to go on till two o'clock."

"Twelve-thirty is long enough. Besides, I told her we were going on a trip and she has to get ready for it, sort out the things she wants to take along, pack."

"You told her before you told me."

"I told you last week, darling."

"I must be going crazy," said Kitty, as he drove through their gate. "I forgot all about it, though I think I packed our bags right then. How can you be so calm about it?"

"Would it help to get excited? I'm sure nothing will happen."

"I'm not," said Kitty. She got out of the car and turned on all the lights that lit up the gate, the driveway, the path to the house and even shone quite a distance into their neighbor's garden, who had complained about the strong lights shining into the bedrooms and keeping the dogs awake. After a while, undressed, bathed, and having taken a valium, she came down again to the swimming pool where Kent was having his goodnight swim.

"Wonderful," he said. "I hope you brought a nightcap with you. We can sit here. It's warm enough. Are you warm? We can wait for them here."

Twenty minutes later Kitty said, "It's twelve-thirty."

Kent, who had been checking his waterproof watch, laughed. "Sweet, it would take Kate five to fifteen minutes to get here, and remember what youngsters are like. They stand around saying goodbye forever, and thank you a thousand times, and then start a discussion, who's going to take who home, who could drop somebody on his way, and all the silly problems — what girl or boy wants to spend a little more time with this or that boy or girl. It can take a good hour."

"Not with Miss Brown there."

"Even with Miss Brown there."

He went into the house to get a coverlet for Kitty, debated if he should bring her another drink even though he knew that alcohol would counteract the sedative she had taken, decided to let her decide and took drinks for both of them. Before returning to the swimming pool, he

170

walked up the driveway to the gate. The road lay ahead, dark and empty. He told himself that he had done everything in his power, gone to the F.B.I., engaged a private detective, and when Ward had been murdered, accepted the people recommended by the F.B.I. to watch over his daughter. Not that any of it had been successful, and there was still no trace of Jacob Summerfield. But according to the ultimatum there were still two full days, forty-eight hours before the maniac would act, if he acted at all, and by that time they would be out of the country. He had even taken the precaution to register himself, Kitty and Kate under another name.

There was a sound like a shot, and for a moment Kent froze. He went back to Kitty. "Did you hear that noise?" she asked.

"Probably a tyre blowing."

"What's the time?"

"One."

"Why didn't Miss Brown phone?"

"Probably because there was no reason to call. Just as I told you — the usual delays."

Ten minutes later they heard the roar of a motor bike. Jerry, with his helmet on. He almost drove the bike into the pool before he managed to bring it to a screeching stop. "Is Kate home?"

"Kate?"

"She got into the Lincoln Eddie Travers drives, his parents' car. They were going home with somebody else, and they let that shit have their Lincoln, and Kate said she'd never driven in a Lincoln, and I was a pig to resent it. I followed them but they were faster and veered off and I lost them. You're sure Kate isn't home?"

"Let's go in," said Kitty. She was already running toward the house. Kent followed her. Jerry called after them, "Give me a ring when she comes in. I'll be sitting by the phone, so don't be afraid to disturb my parents."

When they got into the house, Kitty asked again, "What time is it?" She lighted a cigarette, stubbed it out, lighted another. It was then that Miss Brown and Bartlett arrived.

171

"Where is Kate?" Kitty couldn't keep her voice from rising.

"Gone off with Eddie Travers in a Lincoln," said bartlett.

"What a sly one she is," said Miss Brown. "We went to the ladies room together. I heard her lock the door, but when I came out it was open. I'm going to resign. I seem to have lost my grip."

"We just caught a glimpse of her getting into the Lincoln which took off like a bat out of hell. Miss Brown shot twice but both fell short of the speeding car. We followed them to the Parkway where we lost them in traffic."

"My God," cried Kitty. "Eddie could have lost control of the car. Kate could have been killed."

Barlett ignored the outburst. "We phoned the police from the next booth, then we drove to the Travers' place. They'd gone to bed. No, Eddie wan't home yet. Nothing to worry about, they said. He often took a girl for a drive and turned up when he pleased. They said there was no way they could impose any authority on him. He's going on nineteen and always makes sure the girl is on the pill."

It was then that Kitty fainted. Miss Brown picked her up with one quick movement, slung her over her shoulder and carried her upstairs. "Go to bed, Mr. Kent," said Bartlett. "The police are alerted. Roadblocks all over the place now. Everybody has the plate number. There may be a call any minute. I'm going to sit up and wait for it. Nothing any of us can do, right now, but wait. Try to get some sleep."

32

SLEEP?

There had been only a few nights in Kent's life when he had been unable to sleep. Some because of pain, until a morphine injection had finally eased it; the night Kitty had struggled for almost two days to give birth to Kate and the doctor had told him they might not be able to save the baby; another night after the morning when, training to jump, his parachute had opened only at the very last moment, and then the night after the crash, no, not after the crash, but after he had received the letter. A nightmare. He was having a nightmare now, wide-awake. Where was Kate? What had happened to her? Impossible to think that Kate had wanted Eddie Travers to make love to her because he was so good looking and already a young man. Kent looked at his watch. The hands didn't seem to move. At about three o'clock, Kent got up and tiptoed into Kitty's room. She was lying on her back, her hands folded across her breasts, like someone dead, but she was snoring slightly, mercifully asleep. Miss Brown must have taken care of that.

He went downstairs. Miss Brown and Bartlett were in the kitchen, sitting around the white table he had made himself and painted with a shiny gloss, resistant to all stains and rings. Miss Brown had laid out a deck of cards. It reminded Kent of the evening he had gone with Sam Slew to see Bill Ward. Bill Ward was dead. Kate . . .

"I always play solitaire when I'm tense," Miss Brown told him. "It gives your hands something to do and clears your mind at the same time. Started it when I stopped smoking. Other people chew gum, and quite a lot take to drink."

Bartlett was knitting what looked like a potholder. Kent

had seen too many people, particularly retired army and navy men, take to some sort of handicraft to be surprised. But Bartlett seemed too young to be occupying himself with knitting needles and a ball of yarn. Both were drinking coffee.

"Police got Eddie Travers an hour ago," he said. "He was parking his car outside his garage. Took him to the station. I went over as soon as the call came through."

Kent hadn't heard the phone ring nor a car starting in the driveway. "Why wasn't I told? Why didn't you call me?"

"Nothing you could have done," Bartlett said. "The boy denied having heard my siren or, as he said, he would have pulled to the side immediately."

"Kate? Where is she? What did he say about Kate?"

"He said that it had been his intention to make love to her, and that he had driven his car to a spot he was familiar with, we presume for similar purposes, but as soon as he tried to make her, she managed somehow to get away, opened the door of the car and ran into the dark. He wasn't able to catch her. Went back to his car and waited. For quite a while. Yelled himself hoarse, says he, calling her. But she didn't turn up. Might have hidden herself, he thinks, and still be hiding, or trying to make her way back on foot."

"Where did this happen?"

Bartlett drew a diagram for Kent, showing the highway, the exit to the cross-country road and the spot Eddie had described, facing the sound. Kent turned abruptly. Miss Brown reshuffled her cards. "Where are you going?"

"To find my daughter."

"The police are swarming over that entire area."

"She mightn't let herself be taken by the police, but she knows my car, and that I honk five times — three long, two short – when I want her urgently."

Bartlett looked up, dropped a stitch, tried to pick it up as he said in his slow, calm voice, "Better stay here. We've put a call through to the F.B.I. that the girl's without surveillance."

Miss Brown got up, went to the stove and put the

kettle on. "Let's not assume the worst," she said. "I'm sure Eddie Travers is speaking the truth and that Kate escaped him when she found out he wanted more than just a little necking." She measured out the coffee like a stingy housewife. "When all this is over, I'm going to give you a present. An electric coffee grinder. The only coffee that's drinkable is made with freshly ground beans."

Kent didn't leave. Instead he opened one of the cupboards, took out a full bottle of whiskey, unscrewed the top. He didn't bother to get ice or a glass, but drank the liquor neat, tilting the bottle to his mouth. "How is it I didn't hear you two talking? Cars driving in and out? The phone ringing?"

"You were asleep."

But he hadn't been asleep. Or had the exhaustion of his emotions got the upper hand of his body? "I should have gone to see Mrs. Johnson long ago," he said. "And Cramer in Newark."

"They've been under surveillance since you handed over the first letter." Miss Brown reached for the whiskey and took a swallow from the bottle, as Kent had done. It made her cough. "Haven't had a drop of liquor in weeks," she said. "Relax, Mr. Kent. Relax. She will be found, and when they catch up with Summerfield, the whole thing will be cleared up."

"My wife doesn't know about his attack on Kate," Kent told her. "And I don't want her to know. She's worrying enough."

Miss Brown turned to Bartlett. "I wish you'd stop that damn knitting. Makes me nervous."

Bartlett laughed. "You've got too many male hormones, B."

Before Miss Brown could parry that, there was a sudden noise upstairs. All three got up, but it was only Kitty, clinging to the banister of the stairs that led from the second floor to the kitchen. Whatever Miss Brown had given her to sleep had worn off. Her voice was perfectly calm, almost like the old Kitty who could rise with equanimity to any emergency.

"Kate has been kidnapped," she said matter-of-factly.

"And I don't believe the police will find her."

"She has not been kidnapped," said Bartlett, "and she will be found."

He moved a chair for Kitty to sit down. Kitty shook her head. "You were wrong, Kent," she said, her voice still steady and cold. "You thought we had two days left, but you were wrong. They've got Kate." She reached for the telephone on the wall beside the door.

"Who are you going to call?"

"The gypsy," said Kitty. "The lady who reads tea leaves. Senora Isabella."

"At this hour?"

"You don't really believe in such foolishness?"

They were all talking at once.

"I don't believe in the F.B.I. or the police," said Kitty. "All of you have failed. It's weeks since Kent took the first letter to the F.B.I., thirteen days since the second one came, and what have you done?"

She started to dial. Kent got up to stop her but Miss Brown laid a restraining hand on his arm. "Let her. The lady will probably be fast asleep and refuse to come over."

Kitty turned around and said vehemently, "Oh, no. She won't be asleep. She feels things long before they happen, and if she won't come here, she'll see me."

Kent could only stare at his wife. He hadn't even known that a woman by the name of Senora Isabella, who prophesied from tea leaves, lived in the neighborhood, much less that Kitty knew her.

Bartlett, knitting furiously, shrugged. Miss Brown reached for the bottle a second time. "Let her. There's no harm in it. I've used those people myself when I was at a dead end. Once or twice successfully."

As she had presumed, Senora Isabella refused to get dressed but she would receive Kitty. Kitty hung up. "Somebody please drive me. I'll just throw a coat over my nightgown."

"I'll drive you," Kent told her.

"Oh, no," said Bartlett. "I'm a better shot than you. You stay here and Miss Brown will watch over you."

Kent had trouble controlling his anger but sense enough

to understand that Bartlett might have a reason to want him at home with Miss Brown.

In much less time than either of them had expected, Bartlett and Kitty were back. "Nothing," said Kitty. "Isabella said she'd had three bad days in a row when she couldn't see or predict anything. All she could tell was that Kate was still alive, somewhere, in a little house."

"In a little house?" Kent couldn't think of one. "In this neighborhood?"

"Not far from here."

Miss Brown got up heavily and went to the icebox. "Let's have something to eat, something substantial, so we can function if necessary. Can I use the steaks that are on the upper shelf? I always put mine in the freezer if I'm not planning to eat them right away. Thank God you didn't."

Bartlett was using the phone, murmuring something about a little house nearby, then he went back to his knitting. "Don't worry," he told Kent. "We'll find your daughter. And if she's in a little house, we'll find the little house. And if she's in it, we'll get her out. Don't worry."

Kent almost hit him, because Charlie Henderson used to use the same words when he was deathly afraid.

"I forbid you to shoot," said Kitty. "Because whoever holds her prisoner will shoot Kate first. She's my daughter, and I wish you'd stay out of it. All of you."

The smell of the broiling meat almost made her sick, and she turned toward the downstairs bathroom when the telephone shrilled. For a second the sound had the effect of rendering all four of them motionless. Then Bartlett picked up the receiver and held it away from his ear so that the others could listen. A low harsh voice was clearly audible in the quiet kitchen. It asked for Mr. Kent. Bartlett passed the receiver to Kent. Like Bartlett, he held it away from his ear. "Yes. Thomas Kent speaking."

"Listen well," said the voice. "We've got your daughter. She will not be harmed if you kill yourself within the next twenty-four hours. No ransom money, you understand? But your daughter unharmed in return for your life. I repeat . . ." Suddenly the connection was broken. "Hello, hello," yelled Kent. "I'm still on the line."

Barlett took the receiver from his hand, put it back, picked it up again, dialed. "Let's try to trace the call. . . ."

"I love Kate," Kitty told Kent, who stood as if frozen to the ground. She began to sob, repeating over and over again, "I love Kate."

Miss Brown took the steaks from under the broiler and put them on plates she had warmed. "Here, let's eat. Steak is so expensive these days. Would be a sin to waste them." But her hands weren't as steady as usual.

33

KATE WAS IN a little house. It was dark inside. She had
been pushed into it, fallen, heard a key being turned in
the lock of the door before she had been able to get up.
Turned twice. And then a car driving away, its motor
whining. She took off the blindfold — still she couldn't see
anything. Her left knee hurt.

Since Kent had told her to watch out for herself and
had given her a flashlight, she had always carried it with
her. Even to the party tonight. She groped around in the
dark for her handbag and after a while found it. She
was relieved to find that the bulb still shone brightly.

The room was sparsely furnished. A sagging couch,
some of its dark brown upholstery torn so badly, the
stuffing hung out. Mice, thought Kate, or rats. Maybe a
cat. She didn't like cats. Their silent way of moving
frightened her, and she was afraid of rats. The Victorian
couch stood opposite a fireplace. Whoever had built it
had done a bad job. There was a rickety table against
one wall and one straight-backed chair. That was all.
She shone her light against the ceiling, which was low. A
bulb, no shade, hung from it. She found the switch,
turned it on, but the light didn't go on. She could just
reach the bulb, unscrewed it, held it to her ear, shook it.
It made the little rustling noise that told her it was
burnt out. She threw it on the couch. She looked at the
windows. Heavily shuttered, with iron bars across them.
She removed one of the bars, but she couldn't open the
shutters which were evidently locked, perhaps also barred
on the outside. A winterized house — "cottage", she corrected herself aloud, surprised to hear her voice echoing
like a ghost's. There was a door to her left. It opened
into a bathroom. A tin bathtub on four rusty legs, above

it a gas burner fixed to the wall. A small wash basin. Neither the faucets above it nor the ones over the tub worked. They just made a screechy sound and let out a few driblets of dark brown water. The water had been turned off. She looked at the only window. It had been barred the same way, so had the ones in the kitchen. The door to the kitchen also led from the living room; a primitive kitchen, no stove, only an electric plate with two burners plugged in, neither of which functioned. So the electricity was turned off too. A refrigerator with the door open. Inside it a couple of cokes and soda water, two loaves of bread which seemed fresh — they were soft to the touch — and some fruit. And there was a trap door. It wasn't locked. She pulled it up and went down the stairs to the cellar, which was empty except for a closet, its ramshackle door ajar. It was filled with tools. Axes, spades, some iron hooks, a wrench, a kerosene lamp, empty and broken near the wick. A jelly jar. She directed her flashlight against the windows. There were three tiny ones, set very low, meeting the cement floor, with iron grills across them. Crawl space, to get to the pipes. Something made a whistling sound. To her right, on a pile of wood, sat a big rat. It looked starved. Kate flew up the stairs and slammed the trap door back onto the floor. But there had to be an attic, even if only a tiny one. She found the door leading to it in the bathroom, and went up the narrow, rough wood stairs. Some old trunks, their leather cracked, and papers bulging out of one. A few candles on the floor, gnawed to a third of their size. She took one, pulled out as much paper as she could from the trunk and carried it downstairs.

If I make a fire, she thought, someone may see the smoke and wonder why there should be smoke coming from a deserted cottage. But in a short while it will be morning and then nobody may notice the smoke. Still she went to the fireplace. A heavy piece of sheet-iron barred the opening. She kneeled for a while in front of it, trying to muster the courage to go down the cellar again to get some tools and some of the wood on which the rat had sat. Five minutes later she was ready to risk the rat attacking her. It was still there. She threw the piece of fresh bread she had taken from the refrigerator toward it, and it left the woodpile to get it, then withdrew across the cellar toward one of the tiny windows. She picked up as much wood as she could carry and a crowbar and went upstairs again. Once more she tried one of the windows, then another, but even with the crowbar she couldn't make them budge. Then she went back to the fireplace.

The iron sheet looked forbidding. Sideways, thought Kate, and pushed the bar she had taken from one of the windows first to the right, then between the bricks and the iron. Slowly, ever so slowly, the sheet moved. Upward. Inside, on the hearth, instead of a grate a few bricks were laid to form a circle. Kate wound the paper she had brought down from the attic around her arm, then placed it on the bricks, the wood carefully across it, the small pieces first, two bigger ones on top. Only then did it occur to her that she had no matches.

Her eyes fell on the rickety table. Its drawer came out when she tried to pull it open. Something fell out of it, slid across the floor. Kate, shining her flashlight all over, found it finally under the dilapidated couch. A small plastic tile with one letter on it. The letter K. Colored in red ink.

Her heart began to pound so hard, she could hear her pulse echoing in her ears. A letter, not handwritten, in block letters, capital letters, like in a scrabble set, on blue paper. The realization that she was in the house of the man who had asked her father to kill himself if he wanted no harm to come to his daughter made her heart race even faster. For quite a while she sat motionless, then she went into the kitchen and took an orange. She peeled it slowly, sucked it, put it back in the refrigerator. Suddenly her numbed mind began to work again. By this time Thomas would know that something had happened to her. And knowing how much he loved her — perhaps more even than life itself — he might do something insane to keep her alive and healthy. She had to get out. She had to think of a way to get out.

She went back to the living room and retrieved the

little red-inked tile, which she had quite automatically put back into the drawer. It was a piece of evidence. She put it in her mouth. Nobody trying to kill her would think of opening her mouth, and if she was killed and found, as she undoubtedly would be, some time or other, it would still be there, and perhaps... The only thing she had to remember was not to swallow it, whatever happened. Somehow the F.B.I. or the police had to find out to whom this cottage belonged. But right now the most important thing was to get out, not just for her sake, but to save Thomas. For by now she was certain that she had been locked up in this cottage, by whoever it was, to force her father to kill himself.

She went into the bathroom. Surely, with the little gas stove above the tub there had to be matches. But there were none. Nor were there any in the kitchen. She began to cry. Never in her life had she felt so helpless, so lonely and frightened. But crying would get her nowhere.

She went back into the living room. Stared at the fireplace which she couldn't use. Or could she? Could she perhaps escape through the chimney? A year or two ago Kitty had wanted a fireplace in her bedroom, which was situated directly above the living room. Thomas and Sam had built her one, using the flue from downstairs. Kate had helped them, and Sam had explained all the intricacies of a well-constructed fireplace to her. There were some, as for instance in his house, that had iron spikes inserted in the flue lining, forming a sort of ladder to go up and down them. But Sam's chimney was big; this was a small one. The most important thing was, how wide was the throat. The flue itself could be eighteen inches or wider, but if the throat... Kate poked with the iron bar from the window until it hit the throat, just below the smokeshelf. Not very far up. She took off her slip, wound it to make a rope, stretched her arms up, with the slip between her hands, but found it impossible to measure.

She left the living room and went back to the attic again, this time to inspect the chimney, hoping it hadn't been built on the outside. Relieved she saw that, like theirs, it had not.

In former times, chimney sweeps would lower a sack of hay or sand from the top of the roof to clean the chimney. It should extend at least two feet above the roof, altogether, measured from the ground, thirty-five feet, to avoid erratic drafts. It took her some time to figure out that the living room was no higher than seven feet, perhaps a little less. She walked up the eight steps leading to the attic. The usual height of steps was eight inches. Eight times eight made sixty-four inches; the seven feet of the living room at the most, from floor to ceiling, eighty-four inches. From attic floor to attic ceiling about three feet. Thirty-six inches added to one hundred and forty-eight inches came to one hundred and eighty-four inches, exactly fifteen feet four inches. That couldn't be right. But after checking several times, she always came up with the same figure. She looked at the bricks. Even if she added two more feet, it would be less of a risk to try to destroy the upper part of the chimney, from attic to roof, than of getting stuck.

She took the iron bar and started to hammer against the bricks. They were brittle, the cement between them was cracking. In almost no time a few of them fell out of place and then, with a sound like thunder, the top ones came down, some on her forehead. She began to bleed. But she paid no attention to it because she could see the sky. She also could see an iron hook.

She took off her dress, the one her father had bought for her, a pretty dress, all lace. If only it was strong enough to hold her. She made a rope of it, coiling it tightly, then wound her slip around it to make it stronger. She threw it up, trying to catch the hook from which chimney sweeps used to hang their bags. Finally succeeded.

The opening was small, but so was she. Sucking in her breath, her feet braced against the remaining bricks, she pulled herself up. A few minutes later she was out on top of the roof in the early grey dawn. All she could see was trees, their leaves moving gently in an early morning breeze. She sat quite still. There was no way of telling where she was. She tried to look for some electric poles but couldn't see any. She looked down at herself and was surprised to see how dirty the soot and blood had made her. She took off her bra, its outlines outlined on her clean skin underneath. She took off her shoes, her pantyhose, her panties. Anyone seeing a naked girl walking along a highway ... where was the highway? Even if they didn't stop, they'd notify the police. A girl walking in the nude. Indecent exposure.

Carefully Kate climbed to the edge of the low roof, jumped to the ground on relaxed knees, stood still for a moment to get her bearings. The rising sun told her she was in the east. In the east of what? She turned around and looked at the house from which she had just escaped. A shack, with a lean-to. But there had been a naked bulb dangling from the ceiling in the living room, a burner, a refrigerator ... so there had to be electricity. She looked up and found the wire, cutting into the sky. She began to walk.

34

Trees, mostly pine and oak, a sandy path. The sand clung to her naked feet. She was shivering in the early morning coolness. From somewhere she could hear the sound of water. North shore? South shore? She had to be still on the island; they hadn't driven all that long. Perhaps Point Lookout? She couldn't tell. Where was the highway? Close to the shore or inland?

She had always loved trees, the different species which made an individual of every one, but this morning she was afraid of them. Someone might be hiding behind one, ready to catch her. Don't look at the trees, she told herself, concentrated on the wire. There was the first pole. How far apart would they be? She didn't know. It seemed as if her mind wasn't functioning; the second pole alerted it again. She began to run, counting the poles as she passed them. Suddenly the trees grew sparser, a small meadow covered with wild flowers, a fenced in paddock with hurdles for jumping, a potato field, cabbages, corn. In the distance the outlines of a farmhouse. Kate ran faster. She'd knock at the door, ask to use the phone. To reach it she had to cross a macadam road. Unexpectedly there was the siren of a car. She stopped dead. A blue car with a revolving light. A police car. One of the troopers in it got out. "Hey, young lady, what do you think. . . ."

"I'm Katherine Kent," Kate told him. "I was kidnapped last night on my way home from a party. My father is Thomas Kent. Our address is Gilbert Road in King's Point. Please radio at once from your car to our police to notify my parents. . . ."

The officer stared at her. The girl didn't seem to be deranged. He took off his jacket and laid it across her shoulders. "Get in the back," he said.

Kate did. She said to the man at the wheel, "I'm Katherine Kent. Please radio the King's Point police or the F.B.I. that you've found me. It's urgent."

"Jesus Christ," said the driver. "You're the girl we're looking for. Any identification?"

"That's a rather silly question," said Kate, "when you consider the way I'm walking around. Please radio."

She listened to the blurred message. "Found a naked girl. Claims to be Katherine Kent, the one we're looking for." And another voice, from far, far away, giving him orders. She didn't understand them all, there was too much static.

"Want some coffee?" said the officer who had got out to stop her, and he passed a thermos across the back of his seat. But Kate felt faint. She had never fainted in her life and it was an unexpectedly beautiful feeling. Even the slight dizziness and her sudden inability to see straight were quite enjoyable. I'm safe, she thought. If Thomas has just had the patience not to do anything disastrous, everything will be all right. She took the tile out of her mouth. By this time it had stuck to her gums at the back and she had to pry it loose. The letter on it was less red than before. She handed it to the officer. "Watch it carefully. Don't lose it. It's very important evidence." And then she really passed out.

When she came to she was at the police station she had passed so often on her bike. She had never been inside. So many people in uniforms, desks, telephones, voices, Miss Brown holding out a robe, Mr. Bartlett patting her shoulder, a man she had never seen before staring at the red-inked tile with the letter K. "Now, please tell us..." And Thomas, picking her up from the floor and holding her close. "Oh, baby, baby..." He had never called her "baby" and Kate felt touched and at the same time a little offended.

"I don't want to talk right now," she told him, feeling the warmth of his body warming hers, thinking, thank God he's alive. "I want to go home and have a bath and sleep and then..."

It was Miss Brown and Mr. Bartlett who persuaded the investigating officer to let her go in spite of all the jazz he raised of how important it was that they should know at once exactly what had happened. "We're taking her home," said Miss Brown, her dark voice droning with authority. "She will talk in a little while, and as soon as she does, we'll pass it on to you. But I insist on taking her home now."

At the gate of the driveway stood Kitty. On seeing Kate she broke into sobs that shook her whole body. Kate hugged her. "Stop crying, Mom, please. I'm okay. Thomas is okay. It would be terribly nice if you'd run me a tub and maybe wash my hair. I'm filthy all over. And don't worry any more. Everything's all right." But everything wasn't all right, thought Kent. What will that maniac do when he finds out Kate has escaped?

Kate got into her bath. Kitty had scented it with her favorite oil. She was just relaxing when Miss Brown came in, without being invited. She sat down on the rim of the tub, pad and pencil in hand. Her questions were sharp and to the point. Easy to answer. Eddie had told the truth, as far as he could. She had run away from him, in the direction of what she thought must be the highway they had left. There was a car parked among the scrub pines, and suddenly a man standing in her path. No, she hadn't been able to recognize him. He was wearing a stocking cap. He had grabbed her, blindfolded her, shoved her into the car and driven off.

"You drove for a long time?"

"It seemed like ages to me. Oh, yes, I was tied, and gagged. And scared to death." She went on to describe in detail the shack and how she had escaped. "If they take you back to where they picked you up, do you think you could retrace your steps and find the shack?"

"I think so."

Kitty had come in. "Maybe she can give you the directions, draw you a map ..."

"I will."

When Kate was out of the bath and dry, she drew a map for Miss Brown. "The farmhouse here, the paddock, the cornfield, cabbage, potatoes, the meadow. And I got out of the woods here. Then followed the wire."

Miss Brown left. Kate was already in bed when Kitty brought her freshly squeezed orange juice, a huge glass. She sat beside her daughter, holding her hand. "Don't be cross if I fall asleep," said Kate.

Kitty sat for a long time on Kate's bed, watching sleep erase the tension in the young, beautiful face. She didn't realize that she was praying, giving thanks silently to some power that had brought her daughter back, whole and healthy.

Jerry called, and Eddie, and of course Anna, but Kent saw to it that Kate was not disturbed. At about eleven, Kent was informed that the shack had been located, in the vicinity of Easthampton. Registered in the name of Jonathan Litch. Kent didn't know any Jonathan Litch. Neither did Kate, when she was up again and they asked her. "You know," she said, "if you hadn't let me help you build a fireplace for Mom's bedroom, I'd never have thought of it as a possible way to escape."

"You're a clever girl."

"First time you've paid me a compliment. I'll mark it down in my calendar."

"Kate," said Kent. "We're leaving for London tonight, as planned. There you'll be going to camp, after that to school in London. We leave at six. Miss Brown will help you to pack, if you like. I guess you'll want to take a lot."

"More than forty pounds and pay overweight?"

"As much as you like."

"And what are you going to do?"

"We're going to have a little vacation together, the three of us, then I'll start my job again."

"I see."

A small silence fell. Then Kate, looking at the ceiling instead of at her father, asked, "And Mom?"

"Mom's going to stay with you."

Kate closed her eyes. It's ruined their marriage, she thought. That damn man ruined their marriage. If only I could make them stay together. She began to pack very slowly. In between she was interrupted by more people, from the police, from the F.B.I. If Miss Brown hadn't been there, she would never have got through filling the three bags with the things she wanted to take along. At four thirty she went into the living room and almost stumbled over some of the luggage that had been brought down from upstairs. "My poodle," she said. "The one Sam gave me. We can't just leave her behind."

"I'll give Sam a ring," said Kent. "He'll come over to pick her up, or Anna will."

"But I want to say goodbye to Anna, and to Sam. They were my best friends, and God knows when I'll see them again."

"All right. Miss Brown will drop you at Sam's. Sam can take you over to Anna's. Phone when you're ready to come home. But don't be late."

Sam's dogs barked, but shut up when they heard her voice. Sam wasn't there, but his housekeeper Aurelia was. She let Kate in. "Tell him it's cooked," she said, nodding in the direction of the kitchen. "All he has to do is warm it up. Bye now," and she left.

Kate walked into Sam's living room and put the poodle down on the couch. The room looked like an office, mostly modern furniture, black leather couch, a low coffee table, cacti on the window sills. They only had to be watered every three weeks. In a corner, an eighteenth century English grandmother clock, looking incongruous, and a rolltop desk, open, with a swivel chair in front of it. Kate sat down on it. There was no time to wait, not if she wanted to see Anna too. She'd leave Sam a note and walk the half mile to Anna's.

There was no pad, nothing to write on. She pulled open the top drawer of the desk. The first thing she saw was Sam's pistol. She took it out because there was some paper lying underneath it. Blue paper. She picked it up, held it to the light, looked through it. It was water-marked. It was the same paper as the letter. Suddenly her hands were cold.

She tried the next drawer. It was locked. On top of the desk, near an old-fashioned inkwell, the ink in it dry, there was a roll of tape. She loosened a piece, slipped it into the lock and managed to open it. It revealed a scrabble game. Inside the box there was, beside the board and the wooden stands, a small green sack. Green felt. She shook out the tiles on the top of the desk. All the letters were colored with red ink.

There was a noise outside. The poodle ran to the door, sniffed, then went back to the couch and curled up again. Kate sat back, listened, her body taut as the string of a bow. Silence. She must have imagined the sound. Perhaps it had been her own heart thumping. She reached farther into the drawer and drew out a book. Leather-bound, with a wreath of colored flowers on the top. "My Diary." She opened it where its frayed silk ribbon marked the last page written on. Her eyes flew across the pages. "Kent is still alive. He doesn't seem to realize that I meant what I said in my last letter. Nor do Kent and Kitty seem to have any idea what she means to me. But I'll have a chance with her once he's dead. She may not marry me, but she'll come to depend on me more and more, as she's always depended on me, and one day she'll give in and become my wife. If it hadn't been for Kent, she'd have married me, but he took her away from me. I guess I've wanted him dead ever since then, subconsciously. Not so subconsciously really. All those years when I hoped he'd meet with an accident. And when he did, he got away alive. Like the dog who killed our sheep. I waited for the dog, just as I'm waiting for Kent, ever since I saw the bodies of his passengers writhing on the snow-covered runway at Kennedy. I often wish I hadn't driven out that night to fetch him, but I couldn't let Kitty drive to the airport, not in that storm, on those ice-covered roads. March storms are always the worst. But I realize one thing — Kent, anxious and nervous as he is, is not going to kill himself to save his daughter but he might if she disappears. So I'll have to kidnap her. I won't let any harm come to her. There's enough food and drink in the shack to keep her alive for a day or two. I feel sorry for her, but I'll make it up to her once Kent is dead. I know she is fond of me, though she'll suffer from the loss of her father. But given time . . ."

"Now Kent will finally realize that the threat in my letter is real. I know he loves Kate more than Kitty and certainly more than his life. If he doesn't kill himself within the week, I shall find an opportunity to kill him. We've done quite a bit of target shooting lately. A bullet can easily go astray, for instance when he goes up to the target to see who's hit the bullseye. I wonder why I didn't think of that before. Maybe my letter wasn't necessary. No. It was. I wanted to torture him, just as I tortured the dog . . ."

Kate heard Sam's dogs bark. Same was coming home. She laid the diary next to the red-inked tiles on Sam's desk.

Sam Slew came in. He was carrying what looked at first like a lead pipe, but no, it was an axe. The poodle ran over to sniff at his legs, then jumped up at him, just reaching to below the knee. He bent down to stroke the animal. "Kate! What a surprise. But what are you doing here?"

The top of the desk obscured what was lying on it.

"I came to say goodbye," said Kate. "And to bring back the poodle. Aurelia just left. She says the dinner's all cooked, all you have to do is warm it up. The poodle needs carrots and olive oil for the first three months, and four meals a day. But I guess you know all that. I'm sorry I can't keep him, but I'm going away. We're leaving for London. I suppose Thomas told you."

"Yes, he did. Do you really want to go?"

"Under the circumstances, I guess it's for the best. In a year or two I might make the Royal Academy."

"I think you're quite an actress already, considering your cool after all I've heard you've been through. Weren't you frightened?"

"Of course I was," said Kate. "What a stupid question for an intelligent man like you to ask."

While she was speaking, Sam was moving forward into the room. The light of the late afternoon sun was slanting into the room, blinding him. He could make out her figure, sitting at the desk, like a silhouette, but not what was lying on it.

191

"The house I was locked into was registered in the name of Jonathan Litch," said Kate. "But I know better."

"What do you know better?"

"It's your shack, Sam. I found a scrabble tile there. Red-inked. I found the rest here," and she pointed. And now he saw.

He lifted the axe. "Don't be a fool, Sam," she told him, in a slow, calm voice. "The police or the F.B.I. would find out if you killed me." She held up the diary.

Sam lunged at her. Kate grasped the gun he had taught her to shoot, pointed it at him, but he didn't stop. She shot. She shot all the six rounds it held.

After their noise there was a great quietness. Kate looked at Sam Slew on the floor. The blood was seeping from his body, but he was still alive. "I would never have harmed you," he said, his voice fading.

Kate reached for the phone. She dialed the police and asked for an ambulance, put the receiver down, picked it up and dialed again. "Thomas," she said, when she heard her father's voice answer, "I've shot Sam Slew. I've already notified the police to come with an ambulance, but I think, if you'd come over ... Please hurry."